"G
lef

S
Na
tab
de
Br
we
fas
tal
an
sa

th

h

Bantam Books by Cameron Judd
Ask your bookseller for the books you have missed

TIMBER CREEK

BITTERROOT

Cameron Judd

BANTAM BOOKS
NEW YORK · TORONTO · LONDON · SYDNEY · AUCKLAND

BITTERROOT
A Bantam Book / June 1989

ISBN 0-553-27405-8

Published simultaneously in the United States and Canada

Bantam Books are published by Bantam Books, a division of
Bantam Doubleday Dell Publishing Group, Inc. Its trademark,
consisting of the words "Bantam Books" and the portrayal of a
rooster, is Registered in U.S. Patent and Trademark Office and in
other countries. Marca Registrada. Bantam Books, 666 Fifth Av-
enue, New York, New York 10103.

PRINTED IN THE UNITED STATES OF AMERICA

KR   0 9 8 7 6 5 4 3 2

This book is dedicated to
Hix Stubblefield

1

That he was a man of the mountains was obvious to all who saw him. Rough-hewn, unshaven, lean, he rode a big gray that plodded down the center of the wide dirt street. The rider had the easy slump of one used to the saddle. The stub of a cigar jutted from the corner of his mouth, and the shadow of the brim of his campaign hat hid his dark eyes. He looked straight ahead.

And yet, he gave a subtle tip of his hat to the ladies who passed him. The men he sized up silently, out of habit, noting their glances and reading their expressions.

He looked very much like any other trail-weary drifter, and such were common on the streets of Henley, Montana Territory, nestled as it was at the foot of the Bitterroot Range. His trousers, made of wool, fit loosely. Leather thongs strapped his calf-high moccasins to his legs. He wore a long-tailed gray coat, apparently of Confederate origin, and beneath it a faded yellow linsey-woolsey shirt. In a holster on his hip rode a .36 Navy Colt, and the boots on his saddle held two rifles. One was a .44-caliber scope-mounted Henry, the other a .52-caliber government surplus Spencer repeater.

CAMERON JUDD

At the low-roofed, bloodred Henley's Pride Saloon the rider stopped. He tied his gray to the hitchpost, flipped the cigar butt to the dust, and walked to the open door. He stood there several moments, surveying the interior, then went back to his horse and unbooted his rifles. Turning again, he entered the saloon.

The Henley's Pride had no piano, no women, not a single spittoon. The interior walls were painted the same brilliant red as the exterior, but in the dim light they looked black. The place reeked of rotting tobacco spittle and stale cigar smoke.

The stranger picked a corner table and headed for it. He leaned his rifles against the wall and dropped into the chair. He tilted it back against the wall and propped one foot on the tabletop.

The barkeep, a nervous young man with HULON embroidered on his armband, skittered around the end of the bar to the table. His wide, childish eyes glimmered beneath thick spectacle lenses.

"Sir, the guns. There's to be no long arms inside. Owner's rule, you understand—not mine."

The stranger tipped back his hat and studied the barkeep.

"Whiskey, son, Kentucky whiskey, if you've got it. Make sure it's a full bottle."

The barkeep swallowed. "Yes, sir—now, if you'll just let me lay the rifles behind the bar—"

"And one of those cigars in that jar yonder. I could use a good cigar."

The barkeep again swallowed, and his eyes grew wider yet. He trotted obediently back to the bar, more nervous than before and thankful his employer was not here to see his rules violated so casually.

He returned with a bottle and cigar and popped

2

the cork with much trembling. He hurried back toward the bar.

"Friend."

He turned, and the stranger flipped him a coin. It clinked to the floor, and it took him two tries to pick it up. He blurted thanks and slid behind the bar, ashamed of his timidity in the presence of this man.

Sunlight streamed through the doorway; dust and tobacco smoke floated in the rays. The red-stained checkerboard window beside the door, in combination with light reflecting from interior walls, cast a ruby glow across the front of the saloon and a man seated there.

The stranger did not look directly at that man, but studied him in the corner of his vision. The face was vaguely familiar.

The man was slaughtered-hog fat and sported an auburn mustache nearly as broad as his face. He wore a derby, and on his right hip, a Colt. He stared openly back at the newcomer in the corner.

At length the big man rose and approached him, boots clumping loudly on the pineboard floor. He brought his bottle and glass with him and gave it a little wave as he stood smiling in what apparently was supposed to be a cordial manner. The stranger wasn't fooled by the smile; he could read the eyes.

"Good day, sir. May I join you?"

The stranger said nothing, but swung his foot off the table and straightened his chair. With his cigar he waved at the empty chair across from him.

The other man sat down with a grunt, making the chair creak. He poured himself a drink, raised his glass in salute, and downed the hot liquor in a swallow.

"Powerful stuff, powerful," he said. The smile returned, this time accompanied by a subtle tilt of the head. "You're new to town, I believe."

The stranger drew on his cigar and said nothing.

"New—but I've seen you before."

Still the stranger did not respond. He looked past the fleshy face and out the open door.

"Just where, I don't know—could have been almost anywhere. A man in my profession moves around a lot."

He waited for the obvious question. It was not provided. Finally he gave the answer unsolicited.

"Brannigan's my name. Clinton Brannigan. I'm a peace officer of sorts. Mostly, I'm a bounty hunter. You've heard of me?"

Still no answer.

Now the smile drained from the jowled face. Clinton Brannigan leaned forward and spoke intensely: "And you, friend, are Simon Caine—and you're mine."

Simon Caine looked into the porcine eyes. "Don't try it. It'll cost more than you want to pay."

Brannigan laughed. "But my battle's won, Caine! You see, aimed at your gut under this table is the daintiest little Bitterlich you've ever seen, and if you twitch even a hair, I'll use it. You bring as good a dollar dead as alive."

Caine took a drag on his cigar and blew smoke into the bounty hunter's eyes. Brannigan winced and sputtered, but did not move.

"It ain't worth the price, Brannigan. Fair warning."

For a half second the bounty hunter hesitated. His broad lips twitched, uncertainty played through his eyes. Then his gaze hardened again; a cold smile flashed.

4

"Get up slow. Slide the pistol out with your left hand, and hand it over easy, by the barrel."

"Give it up, Brannigan. Walk out with your life."

"Move, Caine!"

Simon Caine's hand whipped to the butt of the Navy Colt as his right foot shot upward beneath the table to pin the bounty hunter's left hand to the underside. The derringer clattered to the floor and Brannigan bellowed in pain, but at the same time he went for his Colt with his right hand. Caine was faster. His pistol boomed and filled the air with blue smoke. Brannigan's end of the table splintered. His bulky form kicked backward and tipped over his chair. He landed face up on the sawdust-and-spittle-covered floor.

Piggish eyes stared in disbelief at the red ceiling, hands groped the air, then his expression went blank and he was dead. There was no sound but the wheezing whimpers of the terrified barkeep.

Caine stood. He looked at the body on the floor and shook his head. He clamped his teeth around the cigar and holstered the Navy Colt, then picked up his rifles and strode to the door.

A man loomed before him, silhouetted against the sunlit street beyond. Caine pushed him aside and walked to his gray. He booted the rifles and unhitched the horse, then swung into the saddle.

The man in the doorway looked into the saloon. He saw the body of Brannigan in the rear, the barkeep pale and frozen like a marble statue behind the bar.

Then he shouted: "He's killed him!"

Caine turned his mount and galloped down the street. He cursed the late Clinton Brannigan. The bounty hunter's intrusion could have come at no worse time, nor rendered impossible a more important rendezvous than it had.

The only good thing about it was there was now one less bounty hunter seeking the price an unforgiving federal government had placed on his head.

He bent low and spurred his horse. From behind came sounds of mounting confusion: men shouting, dogs yapping, women screaming. A man came to the door of the gunsmith's shop and fired a rifle.

Caine spurred the gray again. One more corner and he would be out of town, in the foothills, bound for the mountains that for more than a decade had been his home.

The gray trumpeted and reared as it almost collided with a buggy that came around the corner. On the seat was a young man with a badge on his vest, and next to him a beautiful young woman with a small child in her lap.

Caine was caught between the buggy and the wall of a building. Behind him he heard the man from the gunsmithy coming at a run. There was one way out.

He drew his Colt and aimed at the lawman's face. The lady screamed and drew the child to herself.

There was commotion behind, growing ever closer.

It still was not too late. During the war and many times after, he had escaped tighter spots than this.

But not this time. It would not be the rifleman behind who stopped him, nor this startled lawman. It would be himself—and this lady.

He lowered his pistol and flipped it in the air. Catching it by the barrel, he thrust it butt first to the lawman, who only just now drew his own sidearm. All the while Caine looked into the face of the pale young mother who clutched her crying child.

The lawman took Caine's pistol. The man behind

slid Caine's rifles from their boots and the knife from his belt. Caine raised his hands and smiled around his cigar.

"Mister, looks like you've got yourself a prisoner."

2

In early afternoon a chill swept down from the mountains and clouds thickened on the horizon. Low rumbles of thunder shook the atmosphere. The gathering storm rattled shutters and sent dust demons spiraling down the street.

Town marshal Jim Ballentree put down the flyer he had been staring at and aimed his gaze at the pot of coffee boiling on the stove.

"Hulon wasn't lying, Charlie. It all matches, right down to the scar at the hairline. I can't believe it. Simon Caine!"

Charlie Bradley, Henley's full-time gunsmith and part-time deputy, looked like a man struck ill. A trickle of tobacco juice escaped the corner of his mouth and ran like a tiny brown river into a forest of whiskers.

"No mistake?"

"No mistake."

"You know what this means?"

Ballentree was in no spirit to answer. He walked to the heavy oak door separating the office from the cellblock in the rear. Three cells: two empty, one occupied by a man who to Ballentree had been only a legend.

The door closed behind him with a dull thud. For a time the lawman lingered before Caine's cell, watching the tall outlaw who stood with his back toward him. Caine was looking through the shattered pane of the cell's lone window, which was crossed with rusty iron bars. The cell was dark, illuminated only by a feeble glimmer from a coal-oil flame in a wall lamp. The wind, gusting through the broken pane, caused the flame to flicker and flare, setting disjointed shadows into constant motion on the cell wall. Outside, thunder rumbled more often and more deeply.

"I know who you are, Caine," Ballentree said. "The bounty hunter spoke your name before you shot him." The outlaw did not turn nor indicate he even had heard. In a different tone Ballentree said, "Do you know whose town this is?"

Caine turned and looked straight into Ballentree's face. For a second something in Caine's eyes brought to mind the fierce sadness of a caged grizzly or a treed puma.

"I know." Caine's voice reverberated against the walls of the cell.

"Then why ride into the town of a man who hates you like William Montrose does?"

"I had a reason."

"But the risk . . ."

"I'm used to risk."

Ballentree fished a cheroot from his vest and struck a sulfur match. The smoke drifted across the cell and joined its scent with the dank odor of mildewed stone walls. After a moment's hesitation the marshal offered the smoke to Caine and was slightly surprised when it was accepted. Caine sat on his bunk, leaning against the wall and keeping his eye on the window.

"We're going to have trouble when Montrose finds out you're here. He probably knows already. The barkeep works for Montrose, like everybody else in this town."

"You too, Marshal?"

"No." Ballentree brought out another cheroot and lit it. The tip flared red in the shadowed cellblock. "I got little use for the man, and he's got less for me. I think he was surprised when I was named for this job. Didn't make his wishes clear enough to the town council, I suppose. But that's all to the side. What I'm trying to tell you is that it will take days for the territorial folks to get up here and take you off my hands. And in the meantime, Will Montrose isn't going to sit up there in his big house when he's got his brother's killer right under his nose. And he sure isn't going to be satisfied to let the court have you. Do you understand me, Caine?"

"I understand. Will Montrose will send his boys down here to string me up. Probably scalp me, too, like I done his brother."

The skin on the back of Ballentree's neck tightened. "I always wondered if that old tale was true."

"Not all of them are. That one is."

"Did Robert Montrose really murder your family?"

Caine flinched like a man does when an old wound stabs at him. "He should have killed me too. Instead he just tried to scalp me, but he was too drunk. When I tracked him down, I showed him how to do it right."

Ballentree noted the dispassion of the voice, the expressionless face. Lightning chiseled the line of Caine's profile against the wall. It was weathered, angular, somehow handsome. But dead cold.

"Will Montrose has always bragged about killing

you someday, Caine. I'll do what I can to protect you. It's my duty." He paused. "Besides, you could have killed me out there today."

"I ain't worth dying for, Marshal. You got a fine family. Don't go getting killed and leaving them alone for the likes of me. A family's the most precious thing a man can have."

For a second the coldness melted. Something different touched the weathered creases around his eyes.

"Why didn't you kill me today, Caine?"

The lamp's flame danced in a sudden gust from the window. Lightning flashed again, and Ballentree saw once more that look of intense sadness.

"Like I said, Marshal, you got a fine family."

Simon Caine walked back to his window, and Jim Ballentree left him alone.

Charlie Bradley was scared. His face was pale and his eyes glazed. Ballentree had never seen him look that way before. He realized he was scared too.

"Look out the window, Jim," Charlie said.

Across the street six men stood looking toward the jail. They leaned against the mercantile storefront, smoking and idle, one with his hat pulled low on his forehead.

Ballentree knew them and why they were there. These were Montrose's men, and with their mere presence they were sending a quiet message. A warning.

At length the one with the lowered hat raised it and looked across at Ballentree. Then, with a slow and lazy gait, he stepped from the boardwalk to the street and walked away. The others followed.

"It's starting already," Ballentree said.

* * *

Charlie Bradley shook his head. "No. It's too much for one man. I can't leave you here by yourself."

"You're my deputy, Charlie. That means you got to do what I say. And I'm saying for you to go to my place and watch out for Susan and Joe. I've got a feeling . . . I don't know just what. Montrose might threaten my family to get Caine. Besides, against Montrose's men, two aren't much better than one."

"They'll kill you, Jim."

"Maybe. But I'm the marshal, and it's my job to stay—not yours."

The storm had nearly gone. The pattering of rain on the shingles above declined; thunder rolled like a giant turning in his sleep somewhere over in Dakota. Down the street a dog barked.

Charlie Bradley finally relented. "All right. I'll go. But your wife will skin me for leaving you alone."

The deputy thrust out his hand, a move that seemed awkward as he did it. Ballentree took it; each noted the trembling of the other.

"Take care, Jim."

The door opened and closed, and Jim Ballentree was alone. He loaded a Winchester, then a sawed-off shotgun.

His eyes fell on Caine's two rifles leaning in the corner, and his saddlebags beside them. Hesitantly, Ballentree picked up the latter and sat down on the corner of his desk. He examined the contents, not sure what he was looking for. He found extra ammunition, strips of jerky, some sort of medicinal salve, a bit of cloth with needle and thread, and at last, a photograph.

It was of a woman, quite young, posed stiffly in a fanback chair. She wore a high-collared dress with

12

lace about the sleeves. Her hair was pinned up. She reminded Ballentree of his own Susan.

He dug farther into the saddlebags and touched something he could not identify. He pulled it out.

It was a scalp lock, stretched over a small willow hoop, the hair reddish-brown, the skin scraped as clean as quality leather on the underside.

Robert Montrose. Ballentree's stomach lurched. He stuffed the scalp back into the saddlebag with the rest of the items, then washed his hands.

At the other end of the street lamps were lit in the town livery as silent men gathered. Entering through the double doorway, they regarded without comment the nimbly working hands of the livery keeper. Bent and concentrating on his work, he cast a shadow in the lamplight which was huge and misshapen and in constant shuddering motion.

He stood, grinning without teeth, and tossed his bit of craftsmanship over a beam. He stepped back, admiring his work. The lamps played light on it from their various angles.

"A right pretty noose, if I do say so," he said.

In the doorway a tall man with graying hair and fine clothing nodded approval from atop a big dun gelding. He clicked his tongue and spurred the horse through the darkness toward the massive log house atop the hill overlooking town.

3

Ballentree answered the knock on the jailhouse door with caution, expecting trouble. What he found was a young preacher, clutching a thick Bible.

His sandy hair was close-cropped and he was sunburned. He was quite wet from the recent rain.

The marshal eyed the newcomer, then glanced down the street to the weirdly lighted livery. Phantom shapes of men moved in the doorway. He felt a shudder not entirely caused by the night wind.

"What can I do for you, parson?"

"My name is John Crosston. I'm a minister—Methodist—and I've come to see your prisoner."

Ballentree noted the preacher's accent. British, he thought. An unusual inflection to hear in a small town at the foot of the Bitterroots.

"Why this particular prisoner?"

The preacher nodded toward the livery. "Because he is a sinner likely to stand before his creator quite soon."

Yes, thought Ballentree. With me right beside him.

"I see. Come in."

John Crosston stepped inside, apologizing for the dripping water from his clothes. He looked around the room.

"Got an interest in jail offices?" Ballentree asked.

Crosston smiled. "An interest in anything American, I suppose. I've been in this country less than five months."

"I never thought to see a preacher in Henley. This place is about as remote as the far side of Hades. I didn't figure the Lord would range out this far."

"But he does, though he hasn't gotten the notice he is due. That's why I'm here. I've been sent to establish a congregation. I'm told religious influence is lacking."

Ballentree thumbed toward the livery. "Well, you can bet what that bunch has planned ain't a Sunday school picnic. Preacher, if you're to see my prisoner, I'll have to search you. For all I know, you may be one of them. And you got to be ready to get out when I tell you, because when they work up the courage to come this way, there's nobody gonna stand between them and Caine. You understand?"

"Of course, the presence of a man of God might influence them to—"

"A preacher don't mean jack to them. They got one lord and master, and he lives in that log house on the hill and smokes two-dollar cigars. So when I say move, you move, and don't hang around for benedictions."

"Agreed, Marshal. Now may I see Simon Caine?"

Ballentree searched the preacher, who, with arms and Bible aloft, looked like he was making an altar call at a Missouri camp meeting.

The search produced only pocket change and a small penknife. Ballentree confiscated the latter, then opened the door to the cellblock.

"Visitor for you, Caine. Meet the Reverend John Crosston, come to save your soul."

Caine was still at the window. His expression had been stern, but he smiled when he saw the preacher.

"You know you're done for when the preachers start coming around," he said. "Save your breath for my funeral, padre. Not even you could convince the Lord to take this dirty old soul."

"Salvation is closer than you think," Crosston said. "Marshal, may I speak to him privately?"

"Well—"

"I'm no risk. He does have the right to discuss final matters in privacy."

Reluctantly, Ballentree nodded. "All right. But remember what I told you."

When Ballentree was gone, Caine turned to his window again. Torchlight played across the little strip of street he could see. There were loud and drunken voices. Not long now, he thought.

"What's it like to die, padre? I've always wondered. I've helped a lot of men find the answer to that question. Now it's my turn."

"Don't talk about death, Caine. I'm coming to give you life."

"Then you're a miracle worker. Listen—you hear them? Sounds like they're grouping up."

The preacher spoke in an urgent whisper. "I *have* come to save you, Caine, but not as you think. Jake Armitage and I have—"

The door flew open and Jim Ballentree came inside, his face gone white. "Out, preacher! They're coming!"

Caine wheeled to face the preacher. "Did you say Jake Armitage?"

Crosston was unnerved. He glanced from Ballentree to Caine and back to Ballentree again, and suddenly held his Bible aloft.

"Simon Caine," he said, "if you're to be saved, it has to be now!"

He flipped open his Bible and from its hollowed-out center produced a small Smith & Wesson. In the lamplight Caine saw the glimmer of engraved initials on the butt—J.A. He knew the gun. It had been a gift from himself to Jake Armitage years before.

If Jake was here, there was hope. More than hope, for he and Armitage had dodged fate more times than he could remember.

The preacher cocked the pistol and thrust it into Ballentree's face. "The original idea was for Caine to do this, not me, but under the circumstances, I must improvise. Caine and I are leaving. Unlock the door."

Ballentree's face clouded. "Montrose sent you."

"No. I represent myself. *Unlock the door!*"

Ballentree did, and Caine charged out of the cell.

Outside, the mob nearly had reached the jail. Some of its members wore flour-sack masks. A few carried torches. All were armed.

"Turn your back, Marshal," Crosston said.

"Don't kill him, friend. I mean that," Caine said.

"I've no such intention."

He pounded the pistol into Ballentree's skull. The marshal collapsed.

Outside, someone shouted for the marshal. There was a blur of cursing and dogs barking and the general roar of a lynch mob.

"Damn, there must be twenty of them," Caine said. He pushed aside Ballentree's limp body, and he and Crosston moved into the jail office, crouched and scuttling along.

Torchlight streamed through the windows above the half curtains. Caine went for his rifles and bags. He loaded both weapons and tossed the Spencer to

Crosston. He threw his saddlebags over his shoulder and donned his battered hat.

"Don't know who you are, friend, but I hope you shoot as good as you play preacher."

The group outside, taken aback by the lack of response from inside the jail, surged forward cautiously.

"The outside window?" Crosston queried.

"No. They'd kill us before we were halfway out. There's only one thing to give a group like this"—Caine strapped on his gunbelt, put on his coat—"and that's what they don't expect. Preacher, it's time to get mean as old Satan himself."

With a startling shout, Caine leaped forward and flung open the door, leveling his Henry at the same time. The Henry roared, flame and smoke gouted in the darkness and men screamed.

Unseen by Caine and his companion, a stunned Jim Ballentree let his newly recovered Winchester slip from his hands as he fell unconscious once more. Caine had been in his sights a good five seconds, but he had not squeezed off the shot.

Earlier, Caine had handed him his life. Now he had handed it back again. Right or wrong, he did not know. All he knew was he could have done nothing else.

4

Like dry leaves caught by wind, the would-be lynchmen drew back. Three fell wounded. A few attempted to return fire, then ran. One wheeled and leveled a shotgun. Caine gritted his teeth as he drove a slug through the man's shoulder.

Crosston stood behind Caine and watched, awestruck by his fury. He understood now how Caine had become the legend he was, why he was so feared.

In the urgency of the moment, though, Crosston's awe was short-lived. There was an escape to be made, and that could be done best by running, not fighting.

"Into the alley!" he shouted. "Horses in the shed behind!"

"Not just yet, friend," Caine said.

Caine sent a slug straight toward a man who thrust his head around the corner of a nearby building. The man ducked aside as lead ripped through wood only inches from him.

Except for the four men who lay wounded in the dirt, the street was now deserted. Dropped torches cast an eerie glow upon one of the wounded men as he tried to crawl away. Caine went to him, kicked him over, and hefted him up by his collar. The man whimpered.

"You tell William Montrose something for me," Caine said. "Tell him my quarrel up to now has been with his brother, not him. He's changed all that. Tell him I don't forget and I don't forgive, and give him this." Caine dropped the man and dug into one of the saddlebags on his shoulder. He found the scalp lock and dropped it on the man's bleeding chest.

"He'll know what it is."

Still whimpering, the man nodded.

"Caine, *move!*" Crosston yelled.

This time he did respond. He ran to the alley where Crosston waited, and together they moved to the rear of the jail. Along the street bolder members of the scattered lynch mob reemerged. One followed the fugitives into the alley. Caine spun and fired. The man grunted and fell, clutching his stomach.

Behind the jail was a weeded lot and an abandoned shed. Inside were two horses, one of them Caine's gray. Both were saddled.

"How'd you manage this?" Caine asked as he led the gray out.

"Bought him. It cost me a premium, being the horse and saddle of Simon Caine."

"Obliged," Caine said. Then with a raised hand: "Listen!"

They heard hooves against the street, the creak and slap of saddles on horseflesh.

"Let's run 'em a good chase, preacher," Caine said.

"I'm no preacher."

"I figured."

They rode across a rolling field toward a wagon trail leading into a dark conifer forest. When the pursuing riders emerged into the field, Crosston and Caine were nearly on the other side. Rifles cracked, and lead passed above them like a wailing ghost.

Crosston glanced across his shoulder at the oncoming riders. Then something happened that his common sense told him was near-impossible.

The range, the motion, the darkness—all made it improbable any shot could connect. But by luck or destiny, one of the pursuers fired off a blast as Crosston and Caine entered the woods. The sound of the shot reached Crosston as he saw Caine jerk and fall across his saddlehorn. Even in the dim moonlight, Crosston could see blood streaming down Caine's neck.

Caine's mount veered off the trail. Wet branches slapped the outlaw's face, and he forced himself upright. He was alive. The bullet hadn't lodged, but had cut a long furrow through his skull, stinging like fire and disorienting him. His vision danced and wavered.

He felt Crosston's hand on him, steadying him. Then, somehow, he was riding forward again, faster. His companion said something, but the words were smeared, unclear.

This much he picked out of the jumble: "Up ahead, Armitage waiting with fresh horses." Armitage. The mere mention of the name helped Caine find some reserve strength. He forced himself to ignore the pain throbbing in his skull, and squinted his eyes until his vision cleared.

To the right of the trail some yards ahead was a small abandoned house teetering on the edge of a bluff overlooking a creek. Years of erosion had eaten away the land beneath the house, leaving the back of it hanging over empty space. Log supports had been extended from the base of the house into the bank below in a final effort to salvage it, but apparently its owners had finally given up and left.

"Up ahead the bluff isn't so steep," Crosston said. "We can leave the horses and let them run on, get down the slope on foot and meet Armitage." But Caine heard no more. He rode into a low-hanging branch, unseen because of blood in his eyes. Already unstable, Caine could not recover, and he fell from his mount.

They were in front of the house now.

Crosston's mind worked desperately. He grabbed the reins of Caine's gray and halted his own horse. He dismounted and unbooted the rifles, which he tossed through the open door.

He heard the riders close behind.

He slapped the horses, sending them running down the dark trail. He ran back to Caine. The outlaw had pushed himself upright.

"Come on, my friend," Crosston urged.

Caine struggled to his feet, and with Crosston supporting him, moved into the shack. Both men dropped to the floor as Crosston snaked out his hand toward the rifles.

Only a second later the pursuers passed at full run, following the riderless horses down the trail. Then there was nothing but the sound of their own breathing and the creek waters below.

Gently Caine shook his head, trying to clear the fog. "Good horse you lost me just now," he said. "But you did right."

"How bad is your head?"

"Plowed me good. But I'll make it."

"We've got to get out of here. The bluff is too steep for us to climb down, especially you. But we can't go much farther without walking into the lot of them."

"If we can't climb down, then we'll jump," Caine said.

22

"Jump? Have you seen how high this bluff—"

"*Hist!*" Caine signaled for silence. "Listen!"

Horses. Coming slowly back down the trail. Caine slid to the window. Two riders, armed with rifles.

Caine said, "Always two or three smart ones in every group. They must have figured it out and decided to grab themselves a little glory."

"We'll have to shoot them," Crosston said.

"Not if we can help it. It would just draw the others back. Is there a back way out of here?"

"This house hangs out over the bluff, Caine."

The outlaw moved, stooping, to the back room. He felt the floor.

"Rotten!" he said. He began chipping away at a floorboard, then ripped out the board altogether. Through the narrow opening he saw a ledge of earth just beneath, the drop of the bluff, the creek far below.

Crosston got the idea. He joined Caine and began pulling away floorboards with tense enthusiasm.

The riders approached cautiously.

"We'd better split up," said one. "I'll go in, and you go around the back. I think I hear something in there."

"Be careful."

"Don't worry. I know who we're dealing with."

Inside, Caine and Crosston made the hole big enough to accommodate themselves. Crosston slid through and Caine handed the rifles to him. Then Caine dropped lightly through the hole, stopping to reach back inside to replace the floorboards.

"Caine!" Crosston whispered. He pointed toward the side of the house.

One of the men was coming on foot. At the same

time, the house creaked as the other entered and walked from room to room.

Nothing to do but shoot. Caine reached for his Navy Colt.

He never fired. Above, near the rotted area through which they had torn their exit, Caine heard footsteps. His next move was instinctive, performed with the grace of a man for whom life had been one fight for survival after another.

Caine holstered his Colt and lunged upward. He burst through the hole, sending rotten wood flying. With an animalistic yell, he closed his arms around the knees of the horrified man above and pulled him down through the opening. With a twisting heave, Caine threw the man over the ledge. He writhed as he fell, uselessly groping air, until his body crashed against rock and water fifty feet below.

In the meantime Crosston rolled out from beneath the house and leaped to his feet. He flipped his rifle as he moved and caught it by the barrel.

He swung the rifle like a club into the skull of the man who had approached from the side. The man fell, limp as a corpse cut from a noose.

Caine came to Crosston's side, smiling with approval. Crosston smiled back. Suddenly blood flowed anew from Caine's wound, and he staggered. He might have fallen had Crosston not caught him. A wave of nausea struck Caine, then a burst of fever, and he felt horribly weak.

A rifle blasted, a slug plowing the ground at their feet. The riders were back. The fugitives were caught in the open with nowhere to run.

"We've got to jump," Caine heard himself say.

The moments after that were forever unclear to him. Somehow he managed to make it, with

Crosston, to the edge of the bluff. Whether they jumped together, whether he pushed Crosston or Crosston pushed him, he could never recall. But together they spun out into darkness, bodies plunging to strike the slope about halfway down. From there they crashed painfully over rock outcrops, protruding roots, and dead timber until they splashed into the creek.

5

Two men, a nation apart, were bent to their tasks.

The first was old, his sallow skin, long untouched by sun or wind, almost as gray as his patchy hair. He sat at a desk in a huge drafty house in Boston, putting words on paper in a rushed scrawl. Books and manuscripts surrounded him, old parchments and fragments of scrolls musty with age. Charts and maps and drawings hung haphazardly about the room, tacked to walls and furniture.

Beside the old man's hand lay a pistol and a torn-out newspaper story.

The room darkened as the sun set, and finally the writer paused long enough to light a lamp on his desktop. It cast a small globe of light around him as he wrote. Occasionally he would pause to pick up the crumpled piece of newspaper and read.

When he was finished, he folded the papers and placed them in a brown envelope. He wrote a name and an address on it, and sealed it, then pushed back his chair and walked to the door.

He did not open the door, but called through it. "Lawrence!" His voice echoed, hollow and weak, in the room.

An aging black man came to the door and tried the latch. "It's locked, sir."

"Here," the old man said. He knelt and pushed the envelope beneath the door. "See that it is mailed at once."

"Sir, is something wrong?"

"Go!" commanded the other.

Troubled, the servant left the house, huddling in his coat against a cool breeze. He took many backward glances at the house as he walked, until at last it was out of sight.

He was too far away to hear the single gunshot, the faint echo of which was lost in the clatter of a passing buggy.

At the same time the old man pulled the trigger, far away in the Bitterroot Mountains, another man knelt in a rabbit run and retrieved a rabbit from a snare. Swiftly he snapped the neck and carried his next meal with him to the mountain ridge where he lived.

On the ridge he stopped and looked skyward, mentally sounding a prayer that had no words.

Music in the Ram's Head Saloon was barely on key, but it was enough to satisfy the pointedly unmusical patrons. Two dozen flaring coal-oil lamps swung from the rafters, stained facets casting a multitude of colors against the ceiling.

The saloon was big and boasted a stage with a real lady singer and an orchestra of piano, fiddle, and banjo. Around the area, the common view was that the players sounded better the more they had drunk, or failing that, the more their listeners had.

Sam Mulhaney, the portly, calf-eyed man who owned the Ram's Head, was normally jovial, but tonight he was reserved, quietly but cautiously observing. He watched a man in the corner, an auburn-bearded fellow matching Mulhaney's own impressive girth, but much more solid. His name was Cordell Brannigan, and he had come in a quarter hour earlier, declaring himself ready for a celebration of nothing in particular and everything in general.

Cord Brannigan in a celebratory mood usually meant good business, and for that Sam Mulhaney was glad. But it sometimes meant trouble as well, for Brannigan was a hard man to control when he had liquor in him.

"That Cord Brannigan back there?" a customer asked.

"It is," Mulhaney replied.

"Reckon he hasn't heard?"

"Heard what?"

"Don't you know? His brother got himself shot dead two days ago up in Henley. They say Simon Caine did it, then busted out of the jail, shot up some more folks, and headed into the mountains."

Mulhaney shook his head. Obviously Brannigan had not heard, if his grin was any indication.

"Lord's sake, just don't say nothing to him while he's in here," Mulhaney said.

Just then the saloon door opened and two men stepped in from the darkness. They were covered with trail grime and blinked in the brightness of the room. Cord Brannigan, who had just whispered in a plump saloon girl's ear, roared out a laugh and drew the attention of the newcomers.

After a mutual glance, they strode toward Brannigan.

Mulhaney, smelling trouble, spat a curse.

Brannigan saw the pair coming. His smile remained, but he shifted his attention to them. Locals had a tendency to lay claim on certain saloon girls, and Brannigan assumed the two were coming to defend their proprietary interest in this one.

He whispered again to the painted girl. She glanced at the approaching men and shook her head, then left Brannigan. She laughed as he feigned an attempt to pinch her thigh, while casually slipping his other hand down to the pistol on his hip.

One of the strangers took off his hat and held it in front of him, like a man does when meeting a woman of society or a new preacher in town.

"I'm looking for Mr. Cordell Brannigan. I was told I could find him here."

"Well, that's interesting. Why you bothering me about it?"

The second one answered. "We thought you was him."

"Was, and still am."

Brannigan noted the obvious nervousness of the pair. The first was fidgeting with the hat. A good sign; a man with thoughts of gunplay would not so occupy his hands.

"Sit," he invited. "Have a drink."

"That's mighty friendly, Mr. Brannigan." The two pulled up chairs and sat down. Brannigan reached to the next table and gathered two used glasses. He tossed the dregs to the floor and poured drinks for the pair.

The two accepted the drinks despite the secondhand glasses. The first gulped his drink, the second sipped his.

"This here is Rodney Jeffers," said the gulper, pointing at the sipper. "I'm Johnny, his brother."

"Pleased. Now what do you want with me?"

"First off, let me tell you how sorry we are about your brother."

"What do you mean?"

Color drained from two faces.

"You don't know?" A swallow, a strained voice: "Your brother—he's dead."

Brannigan frowned at first, and then shook his head bemusedly, as if the idea of a dead brother was more novel than sad. "Dead, you say?"

"Yes sir. He was shot down by Simon Caine."

Brannigan leaned back and laughed heartily. "Now, that's one I would have never figured! Imagine old Clinton trying to bring down Simon Caine! Why, he wouldn't be fit to wad Caine's shotgun!"

"We're awful sorry about it, Mr. Brannigan."

"No you're not. Clint was no good to nobody, and he's no loss. I won't waste my time pretending to cry for him." He tossed off a drink. "Simon Caine. Now, there's a hellion. I heard he always stayed in the mountains. Why'd he come down to Henley?"

"Nobody knows. But a young buck helped spring him from jail. Folks figured Caine was getting ready to pull a robbery somewhere."

"Folks are fools. Simon Caine ain't a robber. He's a vengeance rider, and that's all." A realization struck him. "Henley—ain't that Will Montrose's town?"

"Yes."

"Hah! I'll wager old Montrose wasn't too tickled to see Caine ride in under his nose and back out again."

"He wasn't. That's why we're here."

Brannigan pondered the man as understanding dawned. "So Montrose wants me to hunt down Simon Caine for him?"

"Don't rightly know."

Brannigan laughed. "Well, I think I'll have a talk with Mr. Montrose. But I'm bringing some friends with me."

"Friends?"

"The Greenleafs, and Artemus Frye. You heard of 'em?"

"Yes. Mean as sin."

Brannigan raised his glass. "Here's to you, Jeffers brothers. And here's to Will Montrose and Simon Caine—and old Clinton, too, may his soul putrify in peace."

Glasses clinked and smiles beamed, and on the other side of the room Sam Mulhaney thanked the fates for good fortune this night.

Two nights later a party of horsemen led by Jim Ballentree plodded wearily into Henley. Ballentree was solemn, his face whiskered from inattention over four days of riding mountain trails. The band of riders dispersed slowly behind him, heading for their homes, until only Ballentree remained. He rode to the jail and dismounted. Charlie Bradley met him on the porch.

"No luck?"

"No luck. No sign."

"Things have been quiet here. Your family will be glad to see you." Charlie fumbled with the badge on his shirt. It was Ballentree's, worn by the deputy while the marshal was in the mountains. "Here's your badge, Jim."

"Keep it. I don't want it anymore."

"What?"

"I did some thinking out there. About this town and the way so many were ready to string up a man just because Will Montrose wanted it. I'm quitting, Charlie. Turning the badge over."

"Lord, Jim. I didn't expect this. What will you do?"

"Don't know. I'll find something, somewhere."

Ballentree scuffed his boot on the porch. "You know, when Caine was busting out, I had the chance to . . ." He never finished, and Charlie did not ask.

"Take care of yourself, Charlie. I'll be down in the morning to clean out my things."

"Good night, Jim. Good luck."

Ballentree mounted and rode away. Charlie Bradley turned the badge in his fingers, then pinned it back on his shirt. He watched Ballentree's form dissolve into the darkness, then looked up at the house of William Montrose. He could make out six horsemen riding up the hill toward it.

6

In a way, it was the dreams that finally brought Caine the fever. For many nights he had lost sleep to them; for many days he had felt himself slipping closer to sickness. The dreams horrified him, for they were ominous and silent, bearing a message that was never quite clear.

Tonight, though, his dreams were not really dreams at all, but memories.

He was back in his old homeplace in the valley of the Calfkiller River. Nancy's arm was around him, the boy sleeping in his little room at the back. He remembered the smell of Nancy's coffee, the taste of the biscuits she baked him every morning, the warmth of her by him every night.

Tormented by fever, Caine relived in his mind the most terrible two days of his life.

A band of Confederates rode by his farm. A loose horseshoe brought an offer of help, and that was expanded by Nancy into a supper invitation. The hungry soldiers quickly accepted.

Simon and Nancy did not know at the time that at Sinking Cane the Confederates had just murdered a Union colonel who happened to be a close friend of the famed Captain Montrose. Neither did they know that a lone federal had seen the rebel fighters enter their home, and had ridden to Montrose to give word.

The Confederates soon traveled on, riding around a bend in the road and leaving behind only stories of wives and girlfriends and plans for when the fighting was done.

For a day life was what it always was—farming and trading and passing a few moments with Jake Armitage when he rode by in his wagon. Then, at sunset, a drunken and crazed Robert Montrose came charging around that same bend and without warning gunned down Caine and his son, then ran Nancy through with a saber. Young Marcus Caine, crying, pulled himself toward his mother's body and was cut down by the same saber that had felled her. Caine passed out then to the sound of his own screams.

He awakened to pain in his forehead and salty sweat dripping onto his lips. Leering above him, Robert Montrose was attempting to take his scalp. He passed out again as the blade butchered his flesh. He waited for death, but it did not come.

In his fever Caine reached to the line of scar tissue at his hairline.

"Should have died," he said.

Jake Armitage came to his side. He pulled away the groping hand.

"Easy, Simon. It's all right."

Caine heard his voice and was calmed.

Jake. With him through it all. Caine remembered how Jake had come to him and told him that together they would make it right, and then the disappointment slowly building as he realized a war-torn government would do nothing to prosecute, much less punish, Robert Montrose, the Union hero.

Nancy had never cared much for Jake. It was Jake Armitage, after all, who had persuaded Simon to take an occasional drink, to make a few bets from time to time. She saw him as a bad influence and was, at best, coldly polite to him. If Jake ever had noticed, he hadn't shown it.

Others in the community pulled away from Caine afterward, treating him strangely, keeping their distance. Not Jake. He only drew closer, making Caine's burden his own.

Jake was with Simon Caine when he killed the first man in an alleyway in Murfreesboro. Jake was with him through all the others too—the methodical slayings that wiped out the band that had murdered Caine's family.

Appropriately, Robert Montrose was the last to die. He ran hard from the phantom who pursued him, and when he was caught, he died pitifully, whimpering until his heart stopped. Then Caine took his scalp as Jake watched.

Caine and Armitage threw in with the Confederacy when that was done, fighting with bushwhackers and guerilla pistol-soldier bands from Middle Tennessee on out to Missouri. Armitage never left him. He was a brother in arms of infinite loyalty.

Caine moaned and stirred. He opened his eyes. Jake was there.

"You've been dreaming, Simon. You got shot coming out of Henley. You picked up a fever—worst I've seen you get since the time you cut your leg with that poleax. Remember?"

"I remember." He looked around. "Where are we?"

"Old hunter's camp in the mountains. They won't find us. Crosston is on the ridgetop, watching."

Again the fever rose within him. Present faded to

35

past, and in his delirium he saw Jake again, only younger now, as he'd been years ago.

"They offered me a pardon," Jake was saying.

"Take it. You got to."

"All the old Confederates are being pardoned, Simon. All except—"

"I know. Except ones like me."

Jake looked away. "Been some good years, in their way."

"Hard years, Jake."

"What will you do? They'll never stop looking for you."

"Then I'll never stop running."

"But where?"

"Mountains, somewhere out west. I can be safe in the mountains."

"Going to miss you bad."

"We'll ride together again someday, Jake. Someday we will."

"It's a scalp lock, Mr. Brannigan. Taken from my brother."

William Montrose took a sip of fine whiskey as the stocky bounty hunter fingered the rough scrap of hair and flesh. Brannigan studied the gruesome trophy with great interest, but no apparent revulsion.

"You can see why I am so determined to settle accounts with Caine," Montrose said. "A man who could do such a thing is a savage. He deserves punishment, not only for what he did to my own brother, but now yours as well."

Brannigan spoke as if he had been only half listening. "You know, I never saw one of those taken from a man. I hear they come off with a right loud pop."

Montrose looked peculiarly at his visitor.

"Must be as mean as they say he is," Brannigan said.

"Absolutely. A beast, a devil—but a human one. He is as mortal as you or I, no matter what stories people like to throw around. He can be stopped by the right man."

"And you figure that's me?"

"I do. You are a capable man, if your reputation is merited. And that reputation—if I may say so without disrespect—far outshines that of your late brother."

"You can say so with or without disrespect. Makes no difference to me."

"I take it you are interested?"

"If the price is right." Brannigan reached for the whiskey bottle gleaming amber in the firelight.

"Five thousand."

"That's a pretty sum."

"And the equal amount available from the federal reward on his head. Success in this venture could make you a wealthy man, Mr. Brannigan."

The bounty hunter watched the leaping flames. "How will I be paid?"

"Half in advance, half when you bring him in. I prefer alive, but I'll accept him otherwise."

"You're willing to lay out twenty-five hundred dollars and let me ride off with it into the hills? How can you be sure I'll come back?"

"I can't. All I can assume is you will like the feel of that cash in your pocket enough to want more. Bring back Simon Caine and you'll have it."

Brannigan sipped his whiskey. "I won't do the job alone. Them boys I rode in with, they'll go with me. Any objections?"

"Certainly not. You may hire whoever you—"

"Wrong. *You'll* hire them. This is your job, not mine. You don't give me the tools I need, I walk."

Montrose fingered his glass. "My, but you do like to display your brashness," he said coldly. "Well then, who are they?"

"Artemus Frye, for one. You may have heard of him. He'll need, say, two thousand for a job like this. Then there's Morgan Greenleaf and his boy, Billy. Morgan's a good man in the mountains, and as stout as they come. The boy ain't worth much, but Morgan won't ride without him. Morgan'll take two thousand, the boy maybe five hundred."

Montrose said, "You're pushing pretty hard."

"You want Simon Caine, you pay the price. We'll need your best mounts, plus supplies and ammunition. That's the only deal I'll cut."

Montrose tossed the dregs of his drink into the fire, making it hiss and spit. "You've got your deal, Mr. Brannigan. But hear me—if you cross me, if you run out on me, then you're life is over."

"You'll get what I promised you. I don't go back on my word."

Brannigan drained his glass and stood. He slipped his hat on with one hand and extended the other. Montrose shook it, his own hand soft against the burlap roughness of Brannigan's.

"I'm going to enjoy working with you, Mr. Montrose. First thing we'll do is head to Cleek's Station. Old man Cleek knows them mountains better than any, and he'll know where they are if anybody does. I'll be 'round in the morning to see to supplies."

When the bounty hunter was gone, Montrose picked up the scalp lock. His lip twitched. He crumpled the knot of hair and skin in his fist and squeezed it until his fingers were white.

7

As the fever passed and his clotted head wound began to heal, Caine renewed his friendship with Jake Armitage. For the first day, that renewal mostly involved looking at Armitage, getting used to seeing his face again.

"What are you staring at?" Armitage finally asked.

"Something ugly."

"That's mighty rude, Simon. Nancy wouldn't have liked you talking rude to your neighbors."

"She thought you were ugly too."

"Reckon she was right. You were a handsomer catch than I would have been. There was a time I thought of courting Nancy, you know that? Figured to make her my woman."

"I didn't know that." He paused. "But you didn't know Nancy until after I married her."

"That's right."

Caine grabbed the dipper from the water bucket and threw it at Armitage. Both laughed, and years of separation and growing apart disappeared. It felt good to laugh together again, and for a moment they felt as they had years before.

"You know it wasn't supposed to work out like this, Simon. The word got to you wrong. We were going to meet you outside Henley, not in it. We should have never trusted a drunk redskin as a messenger boy. When we found out what he told you, we about died. When I found out you were in jail, I thought I *was* going to die."

"For a while there I thought I was too," Caine said, but the way he smiled let Armitage know it didn't really matter, that he had already put it behind him. "What's this all about, Jake?"

"Crosston will tell you."

"Why the mystery?"

"It's the way he wants it—and besides, I don't really know the whole story."

"Who is Crosston, anyway? And where?"

"Who he is is a man who will make you richer than you've ever been before. He's out scouting around and guarding, looking for anybody on our tail."

"I didn't thank him properly for what he did. Took a big risk getting me out of that jail."

That night Caine did thank the young Englishman, but Crosston let the words roll past, for he had other things to discuss. In lamplight he sat on the fireless hearth and told his story and his proposal.

The light cast his face half in gold, half in black; one eye veiled, the other a jewellike glitter.

"I sought you out for a reason, Caine. There is something I am trying to do, and unless you help me, I won't be able to do it.

"There is something in these mountains that I must find—something lost long ago. Not really lost, but stolen—from my father. He has searched many years for it, and for the last few I have helped him. Now we've found it. I've come to reclaim it."

Caine asked, "What is this thing?"

"Something valuable. A treasure, if you will. But I can't fully describe it to you, for reasons I hope you will understand. Let me start at the beginning.

"My father is a wealthy man, a native Englishman who has built an empire along America's east coast. Imports, exports, shipping, international marketing in precious metals and jewels—he's done it all, and quite successfully.

"He and my mother separated after only a few years of marriage. He came to this country then, leaving her behind. It was as much her choice as his. But my father did not know I had been conceived. He learned of it only after my birth, and sent for my mother then, asking her to come live under his care. She refused. She raised me alone until I was fifteen, then became ill and died. I joined my father, and I've been with him ever since. Though we were strangers for so many years, we drew close upon that first meeting. Today I love him more than any other.

"As I grew, I began working with him, and he taught me a great deal. I also became involved in his hobby—the collection of various antiquities, particularly those of a . . . well, *unusual* nature.

"When he finally found it necessary, he told me of something that had happened to him several years before I came to America.

"In the course of his researches he came across a very covert line of evidence concerning a particular item that had been his chief fascination for years. The bulk of the evidence came from old documents recovered in southern France and shifted into my father's hands by a rather strange series of accidents and coincidences. Other evidence came from ancient British writings and oral traditions handed down through the Freemasons and others.

"He followed that evidence, piecing it together in ways most others had not, and worked himself into the unimaginable position of being able to purchase the very object he had studied for many years. That this should even be possible was a bizarre claim on its face, but my father had reason enough to believe it true. He made the purchase at enormous expense, even for a man of his wealth.

"Few knew of it. It was not the sort of thing one could publicize. There are those who would kill to own it—in fact, many have. There was a time when wars might have been fought over this.

"That, in a way, is what is so ironic about its theft. The culprit was no collector, no secret society—it was my father's own hired man. A *gardener*. A very unusual man—with arthritis, a sickly wife, an oversized son who was totally deaf. He took it one night from the place it was kept and simply vanished with it. My father never knew how he had come to understand what it was.

"I lived with my father several years before he told me of this. He told me for a reason; he had found the thief's trail and wanted me to follow it. You see, his health is failing. He couldn't make the search himself. The trail was not quite complete, so it would take work to follow it up, and my father had grown too old, too ill. I was to complete the trail, find the treasure, and return it to him.

"I agreed, began my search with the few facts we had and added to them. A death record in Dakota showing when the thief's wife died, a bill of sale showing a rifle purchased in Virginia City—that sort of thing. But I never could get close enough. I became frustrated. I began keeping a journal just to ease the tension—it's a habit I now can't break.

"Then, at last, I found the final piece of the puzzle.

"It came from an unexpected source: an Indian legend, told mostly among the Crow and the Flatheads. I heard it first from an old Crow warrior who begged for scraps and liquor outside a fort. It seemed only the vaguest hint at first, until I began examining it, talking to others who know these mountains and their lore.

"It tells of a strange being of some sort—a very large, bearded white figure—who the Indians say guards a treasure in the high Bitterroots. What the treasure is supposed to be varies with whoever is telling the story, but one thing they all agree on: it is somehow sacred and mystical, and supposedly given to its guardian by a spirit, a manito, who revealed himself only as—listen to this—a diseased old man with twisted fingers and joints 'knotty like an old tree,' as my old Crow storyteller said.

"Of course, I immediately linked the legend with the treasure's theft: an oversized white man, a smaller one with an apparent case of arthritis, a mysterious treasure they guard—it all fit. But, obviously, if the legend predated the theft, no matter how well the details fit, they couldn't really relate. So I investigated further, and found the story isn't old at all, but relatively new. I knew then I had my answer. The thief had taken the treasure into the mountains, and along with him his monstrous son—no doubt quite an impressive figure to superstitious Indians and the probable inspiration for the legend.

"Eventually, with the help of an old mountain man, I developed a map to the area where this white 'god' supposedly lives. It's a good map, quite detailed.

"I have it with me today. I believe it shows where

my father's treasure is hidden. It also shows that I need your help, Mr. Caine."

"I don't follow you," Caine said.

"The treasure is in a cave above Sam Ten Pennies' valley."

Caine understood. "Protection," he said.

"Exactly. If I ride into his country alone, or with any guide other than you, the half-breed will have my scalp on his belt within a day. I can't reach my destination without crossing his valley, and I can't cross it unless I'm with one of the few men he calls friend. That's why I searched you out, Caine. That's why I involved Mr. Armitage. Only with his influence could I hope to gain your assistance."

"You're wrong on one thing," Caine said. "Ten Pennies is no friend of mine. He's let me be, and me him, but friends we're not."

"If he leaves you alone, that's enough for my purpose," Crosston said.

"He's going to pay us ten thousand apiece, Simon," Armitage said. "Five thousand up front, five thousand when it's done."

"That must be a right valuable treasure," Caine said. "What makes you think I won't just trounce your head once we get it and take off with it myself? And what is it, anyway?"

"You answered your first question with your last one," Crosston responded. "If you know what the treasure is, its value is immense. If you don't know, you could sell it for pocket change, perhaps, but no more. That is my ace, so to speak, my protection."

"And what if I stick my pistol up your nose and ask you to let me in on the secret?"

"I'd tell you to go ahead and shoot. I'm doing this for my father. I'll die before I betray him."

"Ten thousand dollars, you say?"

"That's right."

Armitage leaned forward. "Will you do it, Simon?"

Caine did not answer. Instead he stood, opened the cabin door, and walked into the night.

Armitage found him leaning against a spruce, smoking. He cut himself a chew and settled it in his jaw.

"The boy didn't know what to make of you running out like that, Simon."

"I don't know what to make of him," Caine said. "That's quite a tale. But I don't trust a man who wants me to help him but won't tell me the whole story."

"That mean you're saying no?"

"A lot depends on you, Jake. You given thought to turning him down?"

There was a long pause before he answered. "I can't."

"Why not?"

"The truth is, he's already paid me—even the pay I wasn't supposed to get until the end. I owe it to him to finish up."

"Just give the money back."

"It's gone."

Caine frowned. "You spent ten thousand dollars already?"

"It was spent before I got it. Gambling debts. The kind of people I owe make this Ten Pennies look like a Sunday school teacher."

"I never would have figured you for a fool, Jake."

"No sermons. I don't want to hear them."

Caine drew on his cigar. "Well, I can't let you ride under Sam Ten Pennies' nose alone. I guess that's all there is to it."

Armitage cast down his eyes, ashamed. But he said: "It's going to be good riding with you again. Just like the old days."

"Like the old days, Jake."

From the Journal of John Crosston

I should be asleep, but it would be useless even to try, I'm far too excited. As I write by the fire, Simon Caine is sitting on a deadfall, smoking, and Jake Armitage already is snoring in his bedroll.

Caine has agreed to help me—more out of his friendship with Armitage than anything else, I believe. Perhaps he feels some obligation to me for what I did in Henley. I shudder to remember that. But I am eager for what is ahead.

Soon it will be in my hands. I will be able to give back to my father the thing around which so much of his life has been centered. I am beginning to realize just how close I really am.

Caine is bothered by my secrets. He has said nothing, but I can tell. He thinks it a fool's venture, and for that I can hardly blame him. The time will come, though, when he will see.

Caine is a strange man, strong, very cold. From time to time there are glimmerings of what he must have been before. Particularly when he smiles, which is seldom.

Armitage is awake—Caine is laughing at him, waking himself up with his own snoring. Now Armitage is watching me write, as he has done so often. I must guard my packet carefully.

Tomorrow we will reach Cleek's Station. Caine told me just a little of it, and I gather it is a grim place, quite dangerous. But we must have supplies, and that is the only place they can be found.

I must rest now. Tomorrow I will be another day closer. Be well and safe, Father. I will bring it back to you, no matter what I must do.

8

Cleek's Station was a brown scab on the land, an out-post for trading, drinking, gambling, hide-selling, and, whenever proprietor Ezra Cleek had some cast-off Flathead maiden, whoring. Beyond the station lay only the tangled wilderness and dark Bitterroot trails.

Caine stayed away from Cleek's, usually, for several reasons. Rumor had it that many who entered to spend the night at five cents a bed never came out again. Furthermore, it was an occasional haunt of bounty hunters and disreputable lawmen. The mountains drew those on the run, as they had drawn Caine twelve years before, and both worthy and un-worthy agents of the law naturally followed.

"I'm a fool for coming here, Jake," Caine said from the ridgetop overlooking Cleek's. "I've got as much a place here as a bastard at a family reunion."

"Then let me ride down and you stay."

"No. A man gets tired of hiding out all the time."

They began a descent toward the jumble of un-painted buildings that comprised Cleek's Station. The place looked much like an oversized lumber pile or scrap heap, the kind where rats live.

"Hold up a minute," Caine said, sniffing the air.

He reined his mount leftward and slightly back, descending now at an angle opposite the Station. At last he led his companions to a wide sinkhole tangled with vines.

"What's this, Simon?" Armitage asked.

Caine dismounted without answering and walked to the sinkhole. He pushed aside the tangle of brush and peered inside. Both Crosston and Armitage caught the stench, a putrid smell on the breeze.

"Some dead critter," Armitage said.

"Here's your critter," Caine responded. He pointed into the hole. The others dismounted and came over to look.

A body was there. The torso was split open and filled with rocks. The obvious intent of whoever had killed the man was to drop him out of sight into the hole, but the body had caught on protruding roots and was suspended in the rocky mouth of the pit.

Crosston went pale. "Who would have done this?" he said.

"Ezra Cleek, son. This hole has swallowed more dead men than hell, and we'd best take care not to become the next ones." Caine removed his cigar from his mouth and tossed it into the hole. "I know that one down there. One-Eyed Charlie Dreyfuss. Injun trader, some of the worst scum in these mountains. Most of the ones Cleek gets don't know better. One-Eyed, he should have."

Caine scouted about until he found a large rock. He hefted it, staggered to the edge of the hole, and dumped it on top of the corpse. The body folded and fell into darkness. Crosston turned away.

Caine shook his head and gingerly touched his wounded scalp.

49

"Shouldn't have done that, Jake. Made me dizzy. Next corpse is yours to sink."

By the time the trio had descended the ridge, Ezra Cleek was standing on the porch of the Station's main building, which served as a general store, saloon, and dining hall for those with sufficiently strong stomachs. He smiled broadly, a welcoming host. Crosston and Armitage eyed him warily, and Caine remained poker-faced. Ezra Cleek scanned the men as they dismounted; his gaze lingered a bit longer on Caine than on the others, but his expression provided no obvious evidence of recognition.

"Gentlemen," he said.

"Howdy," returned Caine.

"Pretty day," the old man said. His head was tilted slightly and his eyes sparkled. Armitage thought of a blue jay. "You pilgrims bound for the high mountains?"

"We're in need of supplies. And something to drink." Caine's eyes narrowed as he noticed that a young man had come around the corner of the building and now stood gaping at them. It was obvious that he suffered some substantial mental impairment, and on his filthy shirt were bloodstains drying from red to rust.

Cleek noted the questioning stares of Armitage and Crosston.

"Don't mind him," he said. "He's my son. He's short—up here." He tapped his forehead. "He can handle your horses, though. Come inside and I'll pour you drinks."

Armitage looked to Caine. The latter stood by his mount for a moment, considering. Then he turned the reins over to the young man and stepped onto the porch.

"We have visitors inside already," Cleek said.

Armitage slid to Caine's side. "Simon—"

Caine cut him off. "I can't dodge every stranger I run across."

The two inside were nondescript enough. One was a huge man, bearded and gap-toothed, dressed in a buckskin shirt and fringed hide trousers. He had a rusting cap-and-ball Colt thrust beneath his belt and a long Bowie on his right hip. As he looked over the newcomers, Caine caught the egg-white gleam of a dead eye. The other man, sipping whiskey from a beer glass, was older, with squirrely, squinted eyes and white wisps of hair. He wore filthy store-bought clothes and a derby hat that had been white a decade before. He slid his eyes over the three who entered; they came to rest on Caine.

The interior of Cleek's Station stank of mold, dust, spilled beer, smoke, even animal excrement. The darkness inside was oppressive, particularly in contrast to the bright sun outside, and the lanterns that swung from the ceiling had to be lit even in the day.

In one corner a hound slept amid a cloud of fleas. In another, a fat Indian girl sat peeling onions and wiping her nose. Flies buzzed throughout the low, wide room.

"A truly remarkable place," whispered Crosston in a sarcastic tone.

"When you got no competitors, you offer what you got and somebody's bound to take it," Caine observed. He walked to the bar, a rough lumber contrivance, as Cleek circled it and pulled from a wooden crate a corked bottle. Cleek dusted it on his sleeve and sat it before Caine, along with three beer mugs.

"I'm afraid my shot glasses are all dirty," Cleek

said. "The Crow girl yonder has been here three weeks, and I can't get much work out of her. She's too ugly for other uses, and too smelly to sell. If you see somebody half blind and noseless, looking for a woman, send him my way, if you please."

Caine sipped his whiskey with the respect the hot liquor merited. The doorway darkened. Henry Cleek entered and slid onto a stool by the door.

Caine gestured toward the bloodstained shirt Henry wore. "Right early in the year to butcher hogs, ain't it?"

Cleek's expression hardened for a moment, then softened again with his fake smile. "That's dog blood. Henry's favorite got into it with a cur earlier today, and Henry held it to his chest as it died."

There was motion at the other end of the bar. The two men there edged a foot closer to Caine and his companions.

"We'll have a pot of stew cooked up in an hour or so," Cleek said. "You are welcome to stay and share it. The afternoon's getting on, anyway—perhaps some beds for the night?"

"Reckon not," Caine said. Crosston sighed in obvious relief. "It's not smart for a man to buy stew where a dog's been killed."

Armitage smiled around the rim of his glass. A faint chuckle came from one of the two at the end of the bar.

"I don't like this place," Crosston whispered to Armitage.

The dead-eyed man at the bar stepped forward, and Caine turned to meet him.

"I know you, Caine," the man said.

"Too bad."

"Will you come without us having to kill you?"

"Reckon you already know the answer to that."

"Yeah." He went for his gun.

Caine's Navy Colt glinted in lamplight, then boomed twice. Two men fell back as if one, the little one dead instantly, the big one writhing for a moment before he expired. Caine turned back to the bar and holstered his pistol. Henry Cleek clapped and laughed by the doorway. The Indian girl kept peeling onions.

Ezra Cleek's first reaction was to thrust out his tongue in a peculiar way and chew on it, making faint squeaking sounds in his throat. Then he squinted and leaned across the bar.

"What's on 'em and in their bags is mine," he said. "Horses too. It's my place, and that's the rules."

"Fine by me," Caine said.

Crosston watched a pool of red spread across the floor.

"We do need us a packhorse, Simon," Armitage said.

"That's so. Cleek, you sell one of these gent's mounts to us?"

"Oh, you don't want what they rode. Cheap bounty killers, cheap horses to match. I've got a good pack animal in the stable. Bought him off a one-eyed trader in here earlier."

"You're a sharp trader, I hear. He probably came out in the hole on that deal," Caine said.

Cleek's lip twitched spasmodically as his mind worked rattishly to assess the comment. After a moment he resumed his usual facade.

Caine negotiated for the packhorse, plus supplies for a long mountain journey.

When they were gone, Cleek had his son drag the

bodies to the door and dump them outside. Then the Cleeks and the Indian girl sat down to their stew.

From the Journal of John Crosston

A long ride today. We've left Cleek's Station far behind, yet not so far as it seems, for we have moved slowly. The terrain is upward all the way, and the horses are considerably strained. The air here sometimes seems so thin you would think a match couldn't burn in it. Already I gasp for breath, but we will go much higher before this is done.

The sky has been clouded today, and there has been a general grim overcast about the land. I've felt restless and disturbed. It began at Cleek's Station, with those two men and the utter calm with which Caine dispatched them. It was fearful, as on the street at Henley, when he left the scalp lock for William Montrose. I heard Caine tell Armitage today he would go back to Henley someday and even the score with Montrose. Caine lives on vengeance and memories.

Nonetheless, seeing Armitage and Caine together, I am inclined to call Caine the more becalmed, the less troubled of the two. Caine has his obsession and his torment, but Armitage has a manner that suggests many regrets haunt him. Certainly he has largely wasted his life. He told me earlier he had never gambled until after he and Caine were separated. Now that they are reunited, Armitage seems happier, though still haunted.

A peculiar thing about Armitage—he seems to define himself in terms of Caine. He seems to have nothing except a connection to a man more substantial, more solid, than himself. Caine is his anchor, his point of reference.

I had an interesting talk with Armitage today when Caine was out of hearing. I asked him if he had ever been frightened by Caine's viciousness and coldness.

His response was a bit more insightful than I would have anticipated. Yes, he said, he has often been afraid of him, but never has feared that Caine would hurt him. "I've felt a fear of Simon like you might feel about a ghost—it's not what he will do to you, but what he is."

There is a powerful bond between those two. Caine would die before letting harm come to Armitage, yet Armitage has that fear of him. Another thing Armitage said might explain that: "I'm afraid sometimes of who he is, and what he is, because I helped make him that way."

That, I suppose, is the phantom that follows Armitage.

Caine also has phantoms. They come out in his dreams. I have heard him call his wife's name in his sleep, and I think he often relives her death. There are other dreams too. I heard him trying to describe one to Armitage only today. He couldn't frame the words. The dream bothered him intensely, and he could not describe it.

My own dreams are not quite as frequent anymore—thank God. I had no choice, yet it bothers me. If there had been any other way . . . but the priest was a threat.

I did it for you, Father, though I pray you will never know of it.

9

The mountain man rode in great pain. The jolts of his mount's hooves hitting the trail stung him with dull jabs of suffering. Blood dripped from two burning holes in his back and a jagged exit wound above his stomach. Somewhere inside him a bullet was lodged, and it moved each time he moved, gnawing away at his insides like a mouse.

Not far beyond he could see a fire. Whose it was he had no idea; perhaps a band of hunters, trappers, maybe Indians—or the half-breed who this afternoon had tried to kill him; who had succeeded, just not as swiftly as intended. He knew he would be dead soon. That is why it hardly mattered whose fire it was. If that of enemies, they could do him no further harm. If friends, then they could take his final message to Opequon, his lady.

Only a short distance, yet it seemed far. He groaned, blacked out for a moment, then caught himself as he began to slide from the saddle.

He pulled himself upright, squinting at the pain. Just a little farther.

It was too late. Darkness spread across his vision, dimming the yellow flicker that had been his mark. Silently the tall man slid from his saddle and collapsed, eyes shut and mouth open. Even his beard was clotted with blood.

His horse nosed his body. The mountain man did not move. The horse's breath came in steamy gusts against his face, but he did not feel it.

After a time the horse wandered farther into the woods and stopped by a little stream to graze.

Four horsemen rode down the dirt trail toward Cleek's Station. Henry Cleek stood outside, alone except for a small kitten that played at his feet, sniffing and pawing a rusty circle in the dirt where two bodies had laid through a cold night, a warm day, and another night—until at last the stench and the flies grew so obnoxious that even the insensitive Ezra Cleek could put off disposal no longer.

At the lead of the four riders was Cord Brannigan, his heavy form swaying in the saddle, as deadweight as a sack of grain. Behind him rode two blond men, both baby-faced, but one considerably older than the other. That they were father and son would have been instantly obvious to anyone with a mind slightly more able than Henry Cleek's. They were Morgan and Billy Greenleaf.

The fourth man had a leathery, sunken look. His tiny black eyes hid beneath heavy brows. This was Artemus Frye; few knew more about him than his name, and fewer dared ask.

The four stopped a few yards from Henry Cleek. Brannigan, chewing a twig, studied the young man and immediately perceived the slowness of his mind.

"Howdy, boy," he said.

"'Lo," Henry said.

"Where's your pa?"

"Up over the hill puttin' 'em in the hole."

Bill Greenleaf gave a childish laugh. "What's he talking like that for?"

"Can't you see, boy?" the elder Greenleaf said. "He's a half-wit."

"Putting what in the hole?" Brannigan asked.

"Them that's dead and been laying here stinking. Pa took 'em to the hole."

Brannigan sighed. "Where is this hole, then?"

Henry pointed up the ridge. "On t'other side."

"And your pa's up there putting dead critters in it?"

"Not critters. Men."

The four riders exchanged wary looks.

"Men?"

"Yeah. Shot with a pistol."

Brannigan then noticed the blood on the ground. "They were shot right here?"

"No, inside. Pa said it was Mister Simon who done it." Henry Cleek knelt, stroking the kitten. "My kitty, she like the blood." He picked up the kitten and held it to his chest.

Brannigan smiled broadly. "Thank you kindly, boy. We'll go see your pa now."

The four turned their mounts and rode toward the ridge. As Artemus Frye rode past Henry Cleek, he reached down and scooped the kitten from his arms.

"My kitty!" Henry yelled. "Gimme my kitty!"

The riders paid no attention. Henry Cleek scrambled up the trail after them. Frye held the kitten high over his head, twisting the flailing little animal to further torment the retarded young man. Henry Cleek began to cry.

Ezra Cleek had just dumped one body when the

four rode into view. Frowning, he eyed his shotgun standing against a tree. He had enough sense to keep away from it, though, and as the band drew near, he put on his phony smile and assumed the attitude of a house servant patronizing his master.

"Cleek? My name's Cord Brannigan."

"I've heard of you, sir. Yes, I'm Cleek."

"My kitty! Pa, he got my kitty!" sobbed Henry.

"We're looking for Simon Caine," Brannigan said.

"Indeed."

"The boy there said he's been here."

Cleek smiled, the face of a senile old minister at a tea party. "Sir, I'm a simple merchant and must sell what I can for my living."

Brannigan fished out a coin and tossed it at Cleek's feet.

"My kitty, Pa!"

"Caine was here," Cleek said. "Two others with him—one older, one a good deal younger and with a strange way of talking."

"When?"

Again the placid smile. Another coin fell in the dirt.

"Day before yesterday, in the afternoon. Caine left a mess behind I'm only now cleaning up."

"So I see. Which way?"

Cleek waited for his coin. Henry was on his knees by Frye's horse, and Frye looked down on him with an almost demonic grin.

Brannigan tossed no more coins, and Cleek figured he had better not press the issue.

"That way," he said, pointing north. "Carrying supplies for a long journey. I know the trail they are likely to follow." Cleek outlined the route, hoping the riders would quickly be on their way.

"Obliged," Brannigan said.

"Pa!"

"Here's your cat, boy," Frye said. He held the kitten toward its owner, then tossed it to Brannigan. Cursing, Brannigan batted it away with his arm and it arched into the sinkhole where Cleek had tossed the corpse.

"My kitty!" Henry pitched forward, face in the dirt.

Frye laughed convulsively.

Henry raised himself and looked around at the group.

"Someday somebody going to hurt you. Someday somebody'll put you down in a hole, like you done my kitty!"

Frye's laughter stopped. He reached for his side-arm.

"Leave it be, Artemus," Brannigan said.

Frye turned to Cleek. "You need to keep better control of your half-wit, old man."

The four rode on. Cleek gathered his coins, bit them, and slid them into his pocket.

"Come on, boy," he said. "Help me dump this last one."

Henry Cleek did not rise. He continued to cry.

"All right, then. I'll do it myself." Cleek was more patient than usual because of the new jingle in his pocket. He hefted the stiff body, grunted, and tossed it into the hole. It disappeared into the darkness and death stench below.

Ezra Cleek said nothing to comfort his son. He walked alone back to the trading post. Henry Cleek cried more, then finally slept in the weariness of grief.

He did not waken until he felt a rough little tongue

against his cheek. Cleek's last corpse had been a ladder out of hell for the kitten. Henry swept up his pet and poured out upon it all the love he could muster.

The rider wore a long cloak that flapped behind him in the stiff breeze and a black derby noticeably inappropriate for these rugged mountains. He progressed slowly, his weary horse fighting both gravity and wind on an upward trek. The rush of chilly air made the man squint and tugged at his impeccably groomed beard.

The man looked big, but wasn't. His face, upon first impression, appeared aged and weathered, yet the prematurely gray whiskers hid skin that was childishly smooth and rather fair.

The trail gradually widened into a road that led into Henley. The rider looked over the little town as he passed through it; the conglomeration of low buildings and false fronts was as ugly as the last time he had seen it. Why William Montrose insisted on living here he could not imagine. He contradicted the thought immediately. Of course he knew why: William Montrose lived here because in Henley his power was unquestioned. The rider felt a swell of familiar contempt, but he squelched it. William Montrose he might secretly despise, but the man's money was something else again.

It was dusk, and light from Montrose's windows streamed out high above the town. The rider's horse pulled to the left, wanting water from a nearby trough, and the man let it drink. "Old Will can wait a minute more, I suppose," he said to the thirsty animal. His voice was soft, but very deep.

He knew he was watched. This was a town of eyes that peeped from behind curtains and shutters, of whispers and suspicions and all other such things that thrived in the shadow of oppression. While the horse drank, the rider swept his gaze across the town, reconfirming his hatred of it.

He moved on again, riding slowly up the hill to Montrose's house. At the stable Rodney Jeffers met him and took the horse's reins.

"Evening, Mr. DeGuere."

"Hello, Rodney. Is he inside?"

"At his desk."

Morrison DeGuere dismounted. "The horse could use some oats," he said as he turned the gelding over to Jeffers. "Fact is, I could stand a feeding myself." He pulled his cloak tighter around him and walked to the house.

Montrose met him at the door. The sallowness of his face and the unusual intensity in his eyes struck DeGuere at once.

"I'm displeased, Morrison. I expected you last night," Montrose said.

DeGuere smiled. "Good evening to you, too, William." He took off his cloak and hung it over his arm. "Your message arrived late, and the ride was hard. I came as quickly as I could."

Montrose wheeled and walked into his study. DeGuere followed. A fire blazed in the fireplace. On the desk sat a half-empty bottle of whiskey and an uneaten meal.

"Have you dined, Morrison?"

"I haven't."

Montrose waved his slender hand over the food.

DeGuere sat down and neatly tucked a napkin beneath his beard. He emptied the plate speedily, yet daintily. When he was done he carefully wiped his fingers on his napkin and poured a glass of whiskey.

Then he looked at Montrose and said, "I understand Simon Caine broke free from jail here."

Montrose smiled bitterly. "Word does travel. He broke free, yes—with help. A young Englishman who told our marvelously ineffective and stubborn marshal that his name was Crosston."

"Crosston," DeGuere repeated, mentally filing the name. "Is he the one I'm after, or Caine?"

"Caine is already taken care of. You might have heard of a bounty hunter named Cord Brannigan. I've hired him."

"Oh yes," DeGuere said. "A capable man, I'm told."

"We shall see. Your only concern is the Englishman. I want you to trace him down, learn everything there is to know: where he came from, what he's done, his relationship to Caine, his plans. I want to know his shoe size and the number of hairs on his hand. Caine escaped me because of him, and I want him."

"You know nothing more than his name—if that is his real name at all?"

"Other than the fact he posed as a clergyman to enter the jail, no. But what more does Morrison DeGuere need, eh? A detective of your skill could do the job with even less."

DeGuere despised Montrose's patronizing, but responded only by raising his glass and taking another sip. "I'll do my best, William." He finished his drink and stood, taking up his cloak. "Crosston—an Englishman. There's something vaguely familiar in that, though I can't quite recall . . ." He paused, slipped on the cloak, then shrugged. "Oh, well—if it is there, I'll find it. What is my time situation, William?"

"Work as quickly as possible. Keep in contact with

me—hire a courier at my expense, if need be. I want to become very familiar, very soon, with young Mr. Crosston."

"May I assume the usual hotel arrangements still hold?"

"No charge for you, Morrison."

DeGuere said his thank-you and went to the door. Montrose called to him, and DeGuere turned.

Montrose looked darkly at him. "Do not fail me."

The detective's perpetual loathing for Montrose surged, but as always, he hid it. "I won't," he said.

"Good." Montrose turned his back on him, and De-Guere walked quickly out the door.

10

Simon Caine raised his hand to halt the others when he saw the riderless horse. A chill swept him.

"Jack's horse," he said.

"What do you reckon, Simon?" Armitage said.

Caine didn't answer. Instead he dismounted and slid the Spencer from its boot. Looking about, he walked to the horse and patted its neck. Then he went farther on, searching the ground as he proceeded.

Before he had gone a hundred feet he found the mountain man lying still and pale on the ground where he had fallen. He was alive, but his chest shuddered with pain every time he breathed.

"Jack. Good Lord."

The eyes, amazingly, fluttered open. The injured man gave forth a weak smile. His voice came in a whispered rasp: "My prayer's answered. Simon."

"What happened, Jack?"

"Ten Pennies." Then he fell unconscious again.

Caine called Armitage and Crosston over to him. "Who is he?" Armitage asked.

"Jack Whitaker. Old North Carolina fellow, from off the Yadkin. This old boy's seen every inch of country between here and there. Just kept coming west with his squaw. She's a Cherokee, name of Opequon."

"You talk like you know him well."

"I do. He's been the only friend I've had since I came to the mountains."

"Who did this to him?"

"Ten Pennies."

Crosston looked sharply at Caine.

Armitage said, "We should build a fire to warm him up."

"No. I don't know where Ten Pennies is. If he's close, I don't want to draw him."

"But Ten Pennies wouldn't hurt you, would he, Caine?" Crosston asked.

"I wouldn't have thought so, but he's never hurt Jack before, either. We may have been dealt a whole new hand."

Caine examined his friend, who was trying to fight his way back to consciousness. He had bled heavily, apparently for a long time.

Armitage shook his head. He had seen many gunshot wounds during the war, and these were severe. "It doesn't look good, Simon."

"I know."

"Why would Ten Pennies do this?"

"I don't know."

Jack Whitaker opened his eyes. "Opequon," he said.

"Don't worry about her," Caine responded. "I'll get you to her."

"No . . . you won't."

Caine knew it was true.

"I'm hurting bad, Simon."

"Why did he do this to you?"

"He's out for white blood—mostly out for Charlie Dreyfuss. Dreyfuss killed Ten Pennies's woman a few days back, and Ten Pennies has been trailing him since. Somehow I got in the way. I was shot before they even got a good look at me. . . . I think Ten Pennies took me for Dreyfuss."

"Dreyfuss is dead now, Jack."

"Dead?"

"Ezra Cleek."

Jack Whitaker laughed at the irony, but pain choked the laughter away.

"Simon, stay away from Ten Pennies. Get out of the mountains, and take Opequon with you."

"I'll see to her, Jack."

The mountain man was breathing hard. The effort of speaking had exhausted him. He closed his eyes.

Caine stayed at his side until he was dead.

They buried Jack Whitaker where he died, piling stones on top of his grave. When it was done, Armitage sang an old hymn in his rough baritone and Caine stood remembering the time Jake had sung that at the funeral of his wife and son.

That funeral had been a time of inward battle, when old values of peaceful living and forgiveness had struggled with a raging desire for revenge.

That day in the church graveyard, the latter had won easily.

His brother, James Brice Caine, had presided over the funeral. The time would not be long before he would deny his kinship to Simon Caine and even change his name to avoid the stigma of being associated with him.

Standing now by Jack Whitaker's grave, Caine wondered what other changes would come.

"He was a good man, Simon?"

"Surely was, Jake. I learned the ways of the mountains from that old buzzard. Never even thought about him dying. He seemed the kind that would stand as long as the mountains did."

Crosston came to Caine and shook his hand. "I'm sorry about your friend, Caine. But we're losing time. We have a long way to ride."

Caine glared back at him. "Didn't you hear what Jack said? Ten Pennies is on a death spree, boy, and there'll be no riding into his country until it's done."

Crosston was incredulous. "We can't possibly give up now! You don't understand, Caine—I have to go on and recover my father's treasure."

"Well, you can forget about it for the time being," Caine returned. "Besides, I got to go to Opequon."

Crosston's temper flared. "I paid you, Caine."

"What's money worth to a man who'll be running the rest of his days?" Caine said. "I'm doing this for Jake, and I'm going to Opequon for Jack Whitaker. If you want me to help you find your treasure, you'll do it my way."

Crosston assumed a haughty tone. "Consider it this way, Caine. If you no longer, as you implied, are protection from Sam Ten Pennies, then perhaps I should just go on without you. The risk would be the same either way."

"You want to go on, then you go on. But Jake stays with me."

"Oh no. Jake is in this to the end, whether he likes it or not, and whatever you think about it."

There was a long, tense pause. Finally Caine said, "You talk about Jake Armitage like that and he's liable to kill you. And if he doesn't, I might."

Caine wondered, though, if what he had just said was true. Jake right now seemed deflated and old. He had taken Crosston's bossing without response. It wasn't something he would have done in the earlier days.

"We'll say no more about this right now," Caine said. "I'm going to Jack's lodge to tell Opequon what happened. You can come with me or ride on—but I advise you to come with me."

Caine's calmer tone soothed Crosston a bit. "Very well. I'll go. But we'll discuss this later."

"That we will."

Caine went to the packhorse they had bought at Cleek's and took off its burdens. As best he could, he redistributed them on the horses they rode and put some on Jack Whitaker's mount. He slapped the rump of the former packhorse, sent it running.

"We can't use this horse no more," he said. "If Ten Pennies recognizes it as One-Eyed Charlie's, that might just set him off."

Caine mounted and the little band rode off in silence.

11

Caine stopped the group shortly before they reached the clearing where Jack Whitaker's lodge stood.

"Something's wrong," he said.

"What do you mean?" Crosston asked.

"Son, someday you'll learn that when Simon Caine feels something wrong, you'd best listen," Armitage replied.

Caine dismounted and unbooted the Spencer. "I'm going in close. You two stay put until I give the word." Then he slipped into the woodland and was gone.

Jack's lodge was a beauty, roofed with dirt and solidly built. Caine had always believed a man's work showed his character, and if that was so, Jack Whitaker had left behind a fine memorial.

At the moment, though, Caine was not thinking about such things, but was instead studying the horses tethered outside the lodge. Saddled and lathered, they had been ridden only minutes before.

Caine dropped behind a deadfall, debating what to do next.

Suddenly a gunshot blast came from inside the lodge, then a shrill scream. The door fell open and a young man tumbled out, screaming again in the same high shriek. He was blond, very boyish, and his chest was a mass of blood.

He rolled in the dirt, arms clutched around himself, giving one screech after another. The shotgun blasted again; a shutter blew outward from the window and showered the wounded boy with shards of wood. Three men came running out the door, dragging with them articles of clothing, boots, weapons. They obviously had been half undressed when the shooting began, and now they looked like surprised lovers exiting a back door as the husband arrived unexpectedly through the front.

Two of the men fairly leaped astride their mounts, but the third man, blond like the wounded one, stopped long enough to heft the latter onto his shoulder and then onto the rump of his horse. Blood streamed down the horse's flanks.

The blond man mounted the horse and put one hand behind him to steady the wounded boy. The others were already riding away by the time the blond man spurred his own mount. At the same time, Opequon came to the door, a shotgun in her hands.

She raised it and fired. The blond man ducked as shot patterned over his head.

When the riders were gone, Opequon leaned heavily against the frame of the door. The shotgun slid to the ground.

She tensed and stooped for it when Simon Caine stepped into the clearing. Then she saw who he was. He thought he saw tears in her eyes—but Opequon never cried.

It made Caine dread all the more telling her the news he had brought.

*   *   *

She accepted it with her usual stoicism, this beautiful Cherokee woman, far from the land of her fathers, in mountains they had never seen. She had come a long way for the love of Jack Whitaker, but now, as Caine asked her if she understood what he was saying, she simply nodded and rose to boil coffee.

When the cups were filled and distributed, she told of what had happened before.

"They came from the forest and entered my lodge. I did not know them. The big one held me while another, a boy, tried to force himself on me. They laughed when I fought them. But I broke free and reached the shotgun. They did not laugh then. They ran like cowards. The boy will die."

"Did you hear any names?" Caine asked.

"The big one's name was Brannigan."

Caine leaned forward in his chair. "Cord Brannigan?"

"He kin of the one you downed in Henley?" Armitage asked.

"Brother."

"Lordy, Simon. That means he must be looking for you."

"Montrose sent him."

"Why do you say that? Might just be because of family."

"No. I know a little about that pair. All but hated each other. It's got to be Montrose. He's hired Cord Brannigan to bring me back."

Crosston sat in silence, bitterly knowing his hope was fading ever faster. Caine was sure to back out. Not only was Ten Pennies a far greater threat than first anticipated, but now they also had hired killers

72

on their heels. Caine would never expose Armitage to such risk.

Only with effort did Crosston restrain himself from smashing his coffee cup against the wall.

Later, Caine spoke to Opequon of Jack's wishes for her.

"He made me promise while he lay dying," he said. "He was worried about what Ten Pennies might do. With these others roaming about now, there's even more cause for concern. They might come back."

"But I don't want to leave."

"I understand that. But I promised him."

"Very well," she said.

They spent the rest of the day at the lodge. Opequon busied herself in minute tasks. Armitage cleaned his weapons and made a repair on his saddle. Caine wandered about the lodge, smoking, thinking, feeling the peculiar emptiness of the mountains. It was hard to believe his old friend was not out there somewhere.

Wagh! We had shinin' times, Simon. Some rough going, but that's how the stick floats. Aye?

Simon Caine smiled to himself. Jack had been mountain man to the core. Knew no other life, wanted no other.

Inside, Crosston fumed silently. He found a corner and sat down, knees up, journal propped in front of him. He wrote furiously, in wide strokes, and his pen often tore clean through the paper.

Opequon had been packing her meager possessions in an elk-hide sack. Now she went to the huge fireplace her husband had built and took from its mantle hooks a gleaming Hawken he had loved. Jack had retired it from use two years before and had always kept it shining clean.

The men slept that night in the lodge, but Opequon was restive. She lay awake, staring at the ceiling beams and listening to the soft snores of Jake Armitage, the clockwork breathing of Crosston. She also heard the moaning and stirring of Simon Caine, who seemed lost in some horrible dream.

She rose in utter silence and took up the Hawken and the supplies she had packed. Without so much as a glance behind her, she slipped out of the lodge and was gone.

12

Billy Greenleaf was alone when he died. Chest ripped open, the boy cried out to his father, his mother, and Jesus as life drained away.

Morgan Greenleaf left his boy because Brannigan had given him two options: "Stay with him and lose your cut, ride with us and keep it." He rode.

The next day, after a night of torment inflicted by what remained of his fatherly love, he mounted and rode back to where he had left his son, hoping to find him still alive.

Billy lay in ivory stillness, eyes half open. Moisture lay in droplets on his white face and in his hair. Mist rose around him in the little grove.

Morgan Greenleaf dismounted and walked stiffly to the body. Kneeling, he stroked back the sodden hair from the boy's forehead.

"I'm sorry, Billy. God, I'm sorry." He gathered up the cool form and held it close.

As if he had come to a decision, he laid the body back in its place and closed the eyes with his fingers. He went to his horse, brought back a slicker, and laid it across the blood-caked chest.

The sun rose above the treetops, sending scattered rays through the forest. A fly buzzed and settled on Billy Greenleaf's face, and the father waved it away.

Finally Greenleaf bowed his head. "God, if God there be, let me pay for what I've done."

He reached, trembling, for his pistol. Sliding it from the holster, he studied it, turning it in the dappling sunlight, looking at its contours and the gleam of the oiled metal. When his courage let him, he raised the pistol to his head.

He closed his eyes. The hammer went back and his finger began tightening on the trigger.

He couldn't do it. He had never been able to do what was just and right. He cursed himself. In a burst of anger he threw his pistol into the brush.

"To desert one's own flesh is a great crime."

In one motion Greenleaf stood and turned.

The man who had spoken was a dark man, almost as black as a Negro. His hair was long and flowed down both sides of his face. With high cheekbones and a narrow Roman nose, he had a distinctly Indian appearance. A hawk's feather was tied to the bright cloth around his head.

Greenleaf stumbled backward. He tripped over his son's body and fell. Quickly he rose again, staring into the face of the stranger, his own face pale as his dead son's. His hand brushed over his holster before he remembered he had tossed away his gun.

"The fear left him before he died," the stranger said. "He died as a man should."

"Who are you?"

"I am Sam Ten Pennies."

Other forms emerged from behind trees and underbrush. Twelve of them in all.

"It is only the greatest of cowards who leaves his own son to die alone," Ten Pennies said.

Greenleaf backed away another two steps, then realized he was surrounded.

"Please, sir, listen!" he pleaded. "I can lead you to others who have money, lots of it. Here—I got some too. It's yours." He dug into his pocket and produced the advance William Montrose had paid him.

The half-breed said nothing. Greenleaf tossed the bills aside. They floated down atop the corpse of his son and scattered throughout the grove.

Ten Pennies gave a signal. The others moved back to their waiting horses and mounted. The half-breed retrieved his own mount from the brush and slid into the worn saddle.

"You may run."

Greenleaf held out his hands. "Please—let me take you to Simon Caine. I can track him down for you. There is a big reward on his head."

Ten Pennies nudged his horse with his heels and moved forward.

"Please don't hurt me! You can have anything you want."

Still the half-breed edged forward. The others followed.

Morgan Greenleaf broke and ran. The two behind him made no attempt to stop him. Ten Pennies did not increase his speed. For a moment Greenleaf thought they were letting him go. Then he realized they were toying with him, giving him a lead before running him down.

As he struggled through the underbrush, sticks and thorns tore at his face each time he tripped over a tree root. But each time he pushed himself frantically up and continued. Ten Pennies and his men were still behind, but moving around the thicket rather than trying to penetrate it.

Greenleaf came to a hill and climbed. Rocks scattered underfoot, and he slid down. He tried again, and this time reached the top.

Ten Pennies now was galloping his mount, leading the others up a clear expanse toward the hilltop. Greenleaf ran on.

He found a narrow gully and dropped into it, running down its course until a deadfall blocked his path. He picked his way through the branches of the fallen tree and found himself in thicker foliage on the other side. He turned. No sign of his pursuers.

Another hillside. He climbed again, until it became so steep that he could not go on. He stopped, looked around, and found another gully, this one apparently carved out of the mountainside by the spring rains. Using protruding roots for handholds, he proceeded to the top.

Still no sign of the half-breed. He took several deep breaths and began running again, inhaling in gulping double gasps, saliva pooling in the corners of his mouth and blowing back to dry on his cheeks.

Trees and brush became sparse, the land more rocky. He picked a path between boulders and conifers, and soon the land tilted up once more. He climbed again, for a long time, then found a cool area behind a boulder and fell into it, panting in the thin air. He closed his eyes.

When he opened them again, he was cold. The shadows lay at different angles. He had slept.

Disoriented, he rubbed his face and stood. He looked straight into the face of Sam Ten Pennies.

Just as before, the half-breed began edging slowly toward the terror-stricken man. Greenleaf wheeled and ran. A sharp stick gouged a hole above his eye. He wiped away the blood and continued.

Then it struck him: Ten Pennies was alone. The others had not ridden to the top. Whether that was the half-breed's design or not, it gave him hope. It was one against one now.

Greenleaf swept up a dead branch from the ground. He turned, crouched like a primeval man-beast, snarling and even faintly growling. But Ten Pennies had moved.

A rustle behind him. He turned; Ten Pennies was there, still mounted. Greenleaf yelled and swung at him with his club. Ten Pennies pulled an Army Colt and put a .44 slug through Greenleaf's leg.

The half-breed holstered his gun and edged forward again.

Greenleaf stood, gritting his teeth against pain, and tried to run. Limping badly, he pushed into a narrow crevice between two massive rocks. Dead branches and scrubby undergrowth blocked his view beyond the end of the crevice. But above he saw sky, clouds—perhaps another open area where he could run lay ahead.

He pushed through the brush. For moment he faced a panoramic view of the Bitterroots that spread out for miles. He turned and saw the barrel of Ten Pennies's Colt. He pushed forward.

The land beneath his feet suddenly disappeared. His stomach knotted as he realized what he had done. Sky and mountains became a whirling blur as he fell off the sheer cliff he had not even seen.

Sam Ten Pennies dismounted and walked to the edge of the cliff. He looked at the crumpled body below, then threw back his head and sent forth a throbbing cry that echoed through the Bitterroots.

13

It could not be, yet he had seen her clearly.

Sam Ten Pennies had seen his slain mate, alive once more, astride a dun and looking at him.

But she was dead, slain by the one-eyed trader.

The half-breed rubbed his eyes, shook his head. But what other woman would follow him and watch him as she had? He knew his own mate, did he not?

Perhaps he was going mad, as Indian and white men alike had claimed. But if this was madness, it was better than a sanity that left him without his loved one.

He believed in spirits and visions, yet he was not quick to accept them. But if this had been a vision, perhaps it bore a message. If so, it had probably been sent by the one entity Ten Pennies considered worthy of his worship.

He stood alone, thinking. In a rugged way he was a handsome figure. Half Crow, half black, Ten Pennies stood out among all categories of men. His life had been one of separation, hatred, and violence.

He had been born through violence. An escaped slave had raped the woman who became his mother by blood, though never by action or love. When he was born, she left him on the doorstep of a hunter's cabin. The hunter, a grizzled old fellow with a slow mind, managed to keep the infant alive on goat's milk squeezed from the corner of a rag. At first opportunity he had taken the boy to a trading post and sold him to a freight runner for three dollars, chortling to the man when the deal was done that the boy wasn't worth "ten pennies, much less three dollars." So it was he got his name.

The freight runner, named Lomax, was married to a sad-eyed woman who gave the boy all the love she could, though repeated beatings from her husband left her unpredictable and sometimes cold toward all around her. As best she could, though, she raised young Sam. He grew up on the fringe of white society, rejected for both his black and red heritage.

Like the woman who served as his mother, Ten Pennies was often beaten by Lomax, until finally he had had his fill of it. He walked into their little cabin one morning with a shotgun and blasted Lomax in the back. From then on Sam Ten Pennies was on the run.

He lived a few years in the Black Hills, then helped herd cattle near Bismarck. There, a brawl over a woman resulted in the killing of two men. He ran to the mountains far westward, drawing ever closer to the Bitterroots. By now his name was becoming known. At least one dime novel rolled off the presses in New York, detailing the cruelties of a character based upon the half-breed.

Ten Pennies fell in with some Crow renegades and at length became their leader. He had shifted northward along the Bitterroot Range by this time and had claimed a broad valley as his own—a claim he enforced with his scalping knife. It was there that he found the closest thing to happiness in his experience, as well as the one thing he had always craved: power. He found also a mate, and then a god he could worship—a figure known only by him and a few others.

He had seen him for the first time upon awakening one morning when the land was bathed in light and mist. That was part of the reason, perhaps, that he believed he had seen a being somehow deified. It was tall, broad, with dark eyes that looked deeply at him. The half-breed had felt no inclination to defend himself, though normally he would have attacked with the first available weapon anyone who came so unexpectedly upon him. He knew, somehow, that this monumental being would not harm him, and so the half-breed merely marveled at him, wondering who he was and why he was silent. But the figure just turned and walked away into the mist.

He saw him twice after that, both times at distances far greater than that first encounter. The last time, one of the renegades with whom he rode saw the figure, too, and that calmed one quiet fear Ten Pennies had suffered: that this strange figure was an illusion, and that he was, indeed, insane.

It was from this companion that he first heard the legend of a large white being who guarded a treasure in the mountains above the valley now claimed by Ten Pennies.

What kind of treasure? Ten Pennies wondered.

His companion did not know. None had ever gone near enough to the white one to find out.

Ten Pennies thought much about the legend and slowly came to the conviction he had found an object of worship peculiarly his own. Gradually he developed his own notions about the white being of the mountains and about his relationship to him. Perhaps he himself was some sort of secondary guardian, charged with protecting the one who protected the mysterious treasure. Ten Pennies thereby created a divine sanction both for his possessiveness of the valley and his killing of most of those who invaded it. He was protecting the One who guarded the secret even Ten Pennies did not know.

There were some who Ten Pennies did not disturb, men such as Jack Whitaker, who had lived long in these mountains and who was no threat to the half-breed. Ten Pennies even now regretted wounding Whitaker earlier on, having momentarily mistaken him for another.

Simon Caine, too, he left alone, for Ten Pennies had heard the stories of how Caine had fought the government of the nation from which he, himself, was estranged. Caine, like Ten Pennies, was an outcast, and also a great warrior, and for that he was left unmolested.

Ten Pennies caught a flicker of distant movement. Her again, almost out of view, now gone among the trees.

Was this a vision? Was his god trying to speak to him? Ten Pennies determined to go alone into the mountains and seek the answer.

Alone in the night Sam Ten Pennies finally surrendered to the mental illness that had seemed ordained for him since birth. That he was of unsound mind had long been clear to most around him—but he had clung to rationality as best he could, and with his will had fought back the advancing madness.

But the loss of his mate had robbed him of that will, and the visions of her since had put an even greater strain upon him. Now, as he let what remained of sanity twist away like a wind-driven leaf, he felt a great unburdening and release. Madness did not seem what it was. Rather, it seemed an answer to the questions raised by the visions of his mate.

He now knew that his god was speaking to him through visions, wanting her death avenged, just as Ten Pennies himself did.

The half-breed arose, his determination made. He would stalk and kill, seeking guidance from his deity through the visions. When understanding was needed, it would come.

He walked higher into the mountains until he came to a pinnacle overlooking spined ridges and valleys deeper than canyons. As when Morgan Greenleaf had died, he sent forth his reverberating cry. It rang through the darkness and echoed back, heard by those who haunted the isolated Bitterroot lands.

Simon Caine heard it and looked up as the echoes faded. Jake Armitage heard it too.

"What in blazes is that?" he asked.

"That's Sam Ten Pennies," Caine said.

"Mighty eerie."

Caine thumbed toward John Crosston, who was asleep, his head on his closely guarded packet. "Too bad he didn't hear it," he said. "It might put a little sense into his head." He looked at the packet. "You ever wonder what he's got in there?"

"Many times," Armitage said. "The time might come when I'll just find out."

"You thinking of taking a look?"

"I am. I want to read that journal he keeps. A lot of answers in there, I'd wager."

"Jake, I've given a lot of thought to it, and there's

only one thing I can do if he insists on pushing this thing. I've got to find Ten Pennies myself and see where I stand with him. And I've got to learn how bad this Brannigan wants to find me. I can't let him endanger somebody else just trying to get to me."

Armitage shook his head. "I can't let you do that, Simon. You need me with you."

"Hang it, Jake, the whole reason is so you won't be with me. Fact is, you're stuck in this until the end. Brannigan is going to hunt me whether I'm alone or not, and Ten Pennies is going to do whatever he takes a shine to no matter what any of us does."

"And if things don't work out?"

"Then I'm dead or they're dead."

"One man don't stand a chance against the kind of odds you'd be facing. There's no way you could survive."

"There's no way I could have survived all these past years, but I have."

"And if I let you ride out alone, knowing what you'll face out there, what kind of a man does that make me?"

"One with sense. Look, Jake, if you and Crosston lit out after that treasure tomorrow, you know I'd be right beside you, probably in just as much or more danger than if I was alone. If we do it my way, one man is endangered instead of three. Besides, I believe I can work out a safe passage for us. Maybe I can get Brannigan or his bunch lost, or steer them toward Ten Pennies and let one end of our problem take care of the other. And if there's a chance to talk to Ten Pennies, I might be able to make a deal with him."

"Reckon there's no point in arguing with you."

"Nope. With Opequon gone, there's nothing keeping me from going out and clearing the way the best I can."

"You think she went after Ten Pennies?"

"I can't figure anything else."

Armitage shook his head. "What chance does a woman stand against a whole band of renegades?"

"Don't underestimate her. She just might wind up with Ten Pennies' scalp. She's as good a tracker and mountain traveler as I've ever seen. I just spent a whole day looking for her sign, and there's no trace."

Crosston stirred and rolled over, drawing their attention.

"You want to wake him up and tell him now?"

"No. Tell him in the morning. That's good enough for him."

From the Journal of John Crosston

I have accepted Caine's proposal. Ten days Armitage and I are to wait here, while Caine goes alone to deal in whatever way he can with Ten Pennies.

His concern for the safety of Armitage is remarkable. The two are like brothers. It was difficult for Caine to restrain Armitage this morning when he left. Jake insisted, despite the agreement, that he go along as well. Finally Jake relented, but if Caine does not arrive back here well within the ten days, I may have trouble keeping Jake from going after him.

We are at Caine's own cabin now, not far from that of the Indian woman who vanished. Caine did not seem surprised when that happened. I doubt we will see her again.

Though hidden away in this cabin, Jake and I are not fully safe. The bounty hunter might come here—

maybe even the half-breed. There is every possibility none of us will survive this quest.

Yet it is worth the risk. Already what we are seeking has cost one life I did not wish to take. There may be others yet to come. But I will return to my father what is his, and if blood is the price, then so it shall be.

Ten days I will wait. But no longer.

14

It had been six days since Caine had left Jake and the Englishman, and in that time he had found only the most meager traces of the half-breed. Caine was beginning to feel the pressure of time. If he was not back in the designated period, Crosston would take Jake in tow and strike out alone, and there would be little probability of survival for either.

Jake, you old coot, leave the fool and get back to safer territory. Don't get killed just to save your pride. Caine barked out the commands in his mind, knowing the words wouldn't have been more useful had he shouted them in Armitage's face. Jake was a prideful man; he felt he owed Crosston, and nothing would dissuade him from paying his debt.

Before he had left, Caine had considered using his own cut to buy off Armitage's debt, but he had never made the offer because he knew it would hurt and humiliate Jake. There was only one recourse, and he was taking it now, though with little success so far.

He caught some sparse sign and followed it through a ravine. Caine picked out the trail as he thought about his years with Jake Armitage.

He remembered the skirmishes they had fought, with handfuls of men dodging in cover and shooting in sporadic bursts. He remembered bigger battles, hordes of gray and blue moving in waves upon each other as cannon roared and the Confederacy sent out a collective rebel yell.

But the war was past. Now all that mattered was the need to find Ten Pennies and, somehow, clear the way for himself and the others.

He rode on, the trail becoming more clear. Ahead, a rumble of thunder called to him.

Caine rode in a hard rain that beat craters into mud and streaked erosive trails down rocky bluffs. It slanted in silver-gray lines and hazed his vision as he dropped from his horse and crouched behind a deadfall, wondering who had just taken a shot at him.

Water gathered in the brim of his hat and sluiced down his back and over his face. His capote diverted some of it, but not all. His feet were soaked and he was chilled. And he could see nothing to give him a clue of who fired the shot.

Another shot spanged off a rock behind him. He ducked, then came up and fired at the spot where flame had flashed. There was movement, then silence.

Caine looked around and above. His position, safe enough from straight-on fire, was poorly protected from above. To his left ran the trail he had been following, narrowing around the side of the mountain until it was a mere ledge above a steep bluff. A similar ledge was behind and above Caine, accessible from several points. He had to move.

He also had to forget about his mount. It was gone, frightened by the shots. Moving on foot was better at the moment, anyway.

Another shot rang, and a voice shouted something

indiscernible. Caine ducked lower and thought out
his plan.

Ahead, where the path narrowed, was a crumbled
heap of rock. The bluff extended above it, but offered
no obvious perch along its face from which a gunman could threaten him. It was no final solution, but
a safer option than staying where he was.

Movement above—Caine wasted not a second. He
threw himself over the deadfall and lunged for the
tangle of rocks. At the same time came a thunderous
sound as an eroding bank, strained by spring rain-
water, gave way. The mountain vomited a white flood
that tore Caine's feet from beneath him and swept
him down the slope.

Daylight vanished and the roaring of water suddenly became a dull rumble around him. He could
not breathe.

Just as suddenly the torrent lifted him back to the
surface in a mass of white foam and brown mud. His
face broke into air and he could breathe again. He
had been swept into a mountain stream far below
where he was before.

Inches above him was a dark mass, moldy and
dank. Daylight streamed in weak rays through some
sort of openings. Caine moved to grasp the
branchlike projections above him. He pulled air into
his lungs and coughed out muddy water. Only then
did he realize he still clutched his pistol. He
holstered the weapon while clinging to the roots
with the other hand. He then used both hands to get
a better grip, and let the water float his body as he
tried to assess where he was.

He finally realized he was beneath a tree, a huge
one rooted in the bank. Above half the root dug into
the dirt, and the other half reached out like a gnarled

hand over the water. He was beneath that portion now, and the dark surface above was the base of the tree.

Water rushed to Caine's chin, splashing into his nose and eyes. He realized he was fortunate to have washed up where he had, for he was hidden from whoever had fired at him. Fortunate, that is, if he could avoid drowning.

He resolved to stay there as long as he could. Let them look for him until they decided he had washed downstream.

There was a noise above him. Some of the light streaming through the root mass was dimmed. He looked. A foot rested directly above him. Someone was standing on the root and looking into the water beyond him.

Water rose to Caine's nose and he had to pull upward a half inch.

"See him?" Cord Brannigan asked.

"No," said Fyre.

"Keep looking. If he washed on down, he'll probably snag up on that dead tree yonder."

Thunder rumbled. The noise of rain pounding the water was intense in Caine's dank niche. Water rose once more, and Caine had to strain to stay above it.

"What's *that*?" Brannigan said. Caine thought he had been spotted. But Brannigan didn't move.

"I didn't hear nothing."

"*Look!*" Brannigan whispered.

Caine had one option. He reached to his knife and drew it. Clinging to the roots with one hand, he slashed the blade upward through the water toward the foot above him.

The foot moved, and Brannigan was gone in a wild rush. Caine's blade probed emptiness, then the water rose past his eyes and hammered his ears.

Caine lunged downward and outward. He came up in the middle of the stream and kicked toward the bank. His foot struck land and he stood. He opened his eyes and shook away water in time to see a Crow renegade, one he recognized from Ten Pennies' band, kicking at him. The foot knocked the blade from his hand.

At the same moment an ax rose and fell, blade upward. Caine dodged the worst of the blow, but his head wound, still raw and tender, was burst open. Blood gushed down his face and he fell senseless.

The Indian flipped the ax blade downward and raised it again. A bronze hand caught his arm.

The Indian turned, puzzled, and looked at Ten Pennies. The half-breed clung to his arm, but stared into the forest. He had seen her, just for a moment.

"Do not harm him," Ten Pennies said.

The renegade grunted a protest and pulled his arm free. Ten Pennies as quickly grabbed it again, his eyes blazing angrily.

"*Do not harm him!*"

Moments later they were gone. Simon Caine's blood drained into the water. Silent as the vision Ten Pennies had taken her to be, Opequon came to his side.

In darkness Crosston stirred and awoke. Only a dim flicker lit the hearth, but in it he saw Armitage, his face masked by shadows.

Crosston also saw the journal in his hand, and said, "You read it?"

"Is all of this true?"

"You *read* it!"

"Is it true?"

Crosston was silent.

"God help us," Armitage said.

15

"You killed a priest?"

"I had no choice," Crosston said. "He would have published his own findings before my father had completed his. The only thing that mattered to him would have been snatched away. And then the Church would have tried to claim the treasure and take that too. I couldn't let that happen."

Armitage spoke wearily. "So all this scheme is something you dreamed up to put your father's treasure back into his hands so he could publish a book? You killed a priest and are letting Simon risk his scalp for the sake of a book?"

"Don't be a fool, Armitage. Can't you see the value of this? The significance? The risks are worth it, even if some have to die."

"Why didn't you tell us about the priest?"

"Damn it, Armitage, I was as honest with you as circumstances would allow. I didn't want you to find out what the treasure was, for just as I told you, its value lies in knowing what it is. You can see that now for yourself."

"Yes." Armitage fingered the journal in his hand. "Why did the hired man steal it? No one ever would have believed him if he had told them what it was. How could he have hoped to profit?"

"He wasn't looking for profit. He didn't steal it for what it is worth, but for what it *is*. He was a zealous fellow, all wrapped up in delusion and superstition. He even left behind a note, written in that arthritic scrawl of his, saying he had been called to guard the thing. That's why he came to a place as remote as these mountains. Protection—for himself and for his treasure."

"Could he still be alive?"

"Impossible. He was old and infirm even when he stole it. He must have died years ago."

"And his son? Gideon?"

"He must be dead too. He had the size of two men and strength of three, but he was deaf, very with-drawn. He probably starved after his father died. A hard death, I'm sure. One his father can take credit for."

Armitage shook his head. "This is all a little too incredible to believe."

"But it is true. There are books, very ancient, that I possess. Books referred to in the earliest poetry writ-ten about the treasure, and long thought lost. They are not lost. And they confirm its authenticity. We obtained them from a reliable individual who also was broker in the actual purchase.

"I understand the incongruity of it all, Armitage. But is it really that surprising? This thing has fol-lowed a path through many nations. To France, to England, and, for a time, to Rome. There are parts of the trail missing, but it can be followed. My father finally found the thing in Spain. He brought it to the United States, and here it will remain after I have re-covered it."

"Back in your father's hands?"

"Yes. And then mine, when he is gone. But I care

little for it, though you may not believe that. I'm doing this for my father, not for the treasure or the glory."

"You killed for your father, then?"

"I suppose I did."

"Does he know?"

"No. He must never know."

"But now I know. How will you shut me up? Will you kill me too?"

"You are a fool," the Englishman said, glowering.

Caine's eyes fluttered open. He saw dim morning light, a network of branches against a pale sky made cloudy by his vision. Pain raged in his head.

Opequon knelt beside him and looked into his face. "Be silent," she admonished when he tried to speak. "You reopened the wound. Rest, and I will take care of you."

How long have I been out? Caine wanted to ask. Hours? Days? But the words never formed, and he dropped away into deep blackness again.

He was in motion when next he awoke. It took a long time to make sense of it, but finally he realized he was on a travois, a makeshift litter slung between two drag poles. Opequon had found his strayed horse, and it pulled him now through the mountains—to where, he did not know. He slept again, for a long time.

Moisture against his lips awakened him. Opequon was giving him water. It was night. He felt as sick as he had after the brutal escape from Henley. He was feverish once more, and as he dropped back into sleep, the dream came again.

It started as always. He and Nancy were together in their farmhouse. He held her close, and she was so vivid and real that he could smell the scent of her hair and feel her in his arms.

Then he heard drums in the distance, growing closer. He peered out the door and saw a funeral procession marching slowly around the bend. They stopped near him and laid a coffin on the earth.

The men who bore it wore hoods, but they threw them back and he saw their faces. These were men he had killed: Robert Montrose and his band, others he had felled in battle, and now some new faces—Clinton Brannigan, and the two men who had died on the floor of Cleek's Station.

In the dream Caine asked who was dead. One of them stooped and threw back the lid.

Usually Caine saw the bloodied corpses of his wife and son in that coffin. But now the dream was different. In the coffin was Jake Armitage.

Caine struggled to awaken, but sickness would not let him. He writhed on the travois, and as always in the dream, something hammered the back of his mind, trying to make him understand a message he could not grasp.

Opequon took Caine to her cabin, and the day after they arrived, the outlaw's fever broke and he was back on his feet. He was weak and dizzy, not really well enough to be up, but he was convinced that Jake was in danger. He tried once to saddle his horse, but collapsed in the effort. His fever came again, and Opequon put him in bed once more.

On the ninth day since he had left Armitage and Crosston, he was well enough to move about. He would leave the next morning, the last morning before Crosston would ride out for the treasure on his own. But Caine felt sure he would reach his cabin in time.

He reminded Opequon of his pledge to Jack to take her out of the mountains.

"I know you want to do for me what you said, but I'll not leave," she said.

"Why?"

"Because of what I must do."

"Kill Sam Ten Pennies?"

"Yes."

Caine shook his head. "It's not the way, Opequon. God knows I'm the last man who has the right to say that, but I also know it's true. Let it go. It's what Jack would want."

"I can't."

Caine did not argue further.

The next morning he rode toward his own cabin, fearing much for Jake's life. He had dreamed again of Jake in the coffin, and though he was not one to believe in premonitions, he could not shake the image, nor the conviction that Jake needed him.

Near his cabin he stopped. There were marks on the earth all about—unshod horses, many of them.

Ten Pennies.

The marks were maybe a day old. Caine mounted and spurred his horse at a run toward the cabin.

Morrison DeGuere, to all appearances, was sleeping. He sprawled across a bench outside a telegraph office, enjoying the shade of the roof overhang. His bowler rested low across his eyes and his fingers were linked across his chest, which moved up and down with the steady rhythm of slumber.

But the detective was not fully asleep. He hovered in a mental twilight between sleep and awareness. DeGuere seldom slept more than three or four hours a night. Half naps such as this one provided the balance of his rest. It was an unusual pattern, but it suited him. Along with a coon-dog tenacity and logical mind, it was part of what made him one of the best detectives from the high plains to the Mexican border.

Even in semislumber DeGuere's mind was busy, sorting and thinking through the things he had learned these past days. Amazing things, even to an old cynic who had seen too much for too many years to be easily impressed. But this John Crosston was fascinating, though DeGuere had not yet decided if he was clever or just very deceived. In either case, he definitely was ruthless—a characteristic DeGuere admired in any man, himself most of all.

He became aware of someone beside him. He opened his eyes and tilted back his bowler. It was the telegraph operator, with a paper in his hand.

"Your associate just wired in, sir," he said.

DeGuere took the paper. "Thank you." The wire operator reentered his office, and DeGuere read the lengthy transmission.

Then he smiled, folded the paper, and nodded. "As I suspected," he muttered. "Just very deceived."

He thrust the paper into his pocket and walked down the street whistling.

16

Inside the cabin was only darkness. No light, no fire. They were gone.

For a moment a hope arose: perhaps Ten Pennies, too, had found the cabin empty. Maybe the impatient John Crosston had not honored the pledge of ten days' wait and had gone on.

When Caine struck a match to light a lamp, though, the hope disappeared. The cabin was ransacked. His meager furnishings were scattered, and most of the food was gone, as were his extra guns and ammunition.

And here, at his feet, was blood.

He had no doubt that Jake Armitage and John Crosston were prisoners, or dead. And with night falling, Caine could not search for their trail until morning.

Despair tugged at his throat. He knelt, feeling the blood. It was dry and rust-colored. The raid must have occurred hours ago, maybe a day or more.

He stepped outside, holding the lamp. He examined the ground in front of the cabin. Hoofprints and moccasin tracks abounded, and more blood. Somebody had put up a fight.

Even in his sadness, Caine let a smile flicker. The

thought of Jake fighting and defiant was better than the image of the weak and aging Jake he had known these past days.

But he was also afraid. Ten Pennies was showing no rationality, no predictability. That he had spared Caine's life back at the river and then had come in violence to Caine's cabin was evidence there was something unstable in his actions.

Caine walked back inside and collapsed on the floor. He was weakened and unbalanced because of his wounded head. He lay on the floor a long time, staring mindlessly at the jumble of books and papers before the hearth. It took several minutes for him to notice what they were.

Crosston's journal, and the other contents of the packet he carried. Except for glimpses of the map Crosston kept stowed inside, the packet's contents had been kept from Caine throughout.

He went to the heap and sat beside it, Indian style. He picked up the journal and began to read.

From time to time he had to look away into the dark cabin, partly to let his straining eyes rest, partly to absorb the astounding things he read.

When morning came, Caine had slept little. He set out along Ten Pennies' trail, which was very clear upon the dew-sodden earth.

Two hours later, unseen by him, two riders topped a ridge at his rear. One of them pointed, and the pair watched him for a moment before spurring their mounts onward and downward, riding in hard on his trail.

If Jake Armitage had ever been a coward, he was not now. Tied to a sapling, stripped of most of his clothing, hurting from the stab wound he had suffered during the raid, he spat and cursed at his captors, particularly the hard-gazing half-breed who led them.

He had overheard the fate they were planning for him and Crosston, and it roused a fury that pushed fear aside.

"Come here, 'breed! Cut me loose and see what I can do to you! Coward!"

One of Ten Pennies' renegades came to him and struck him hard in the stomach. The stab wound, superficial but painful, began bleeding. Armitage winced, then spat defiantly into the renegade's face.

The Indian struck him again, harder. He would have beaten him more if Ten Pennies had not stopped him.

"Do not kill him," said the half-breed. "His talk of a fight is good. A fight to the death, eh?"

The renegade smiled. "I will fight him, Ten Pennies," he said. "I will see him die screaming like a child."

Ten Pennies walked to Armitage and lifted his chin. He looked into his eyes. "You wish to fight the Wolf? You think you can defeat him? And what shall we do with your young friend?"

Crosston looked at Ten Pennies and spoke for the first time since his capture: "I will tell you what to do with me. Let me fight. If I win, let me go free. Give me safe passage through your valley."

The half-breed was intrigued. "Safe passage? For what purpose?"

"So that I may reach the place I must go."

Not an answer, but Ten Pennies did not pursue it. He was thinking. "So you, too, wish to fight the Wolf?"

"No," Crosston said. "I will fight my friend."

Armitage blurted, "Are you loco?"

Ten Pennies was very interested now. "A fight to the death, with the winner to go free?"

"Yes. With a horse and weapons."

"Crosston—"

Ten Pennies chuckled. "You will fight each other. The one who lives has my word—no harm will come to him in my country."

Armitage twisted his neck to look at Crosston, unbelieving. Crosston evaded his eyes as an Indian cut their bonds.

Lashed together at the wrists, Armitage and Crosston were given knives. The band of renegades gathered in a wide circle around the two men, grinning and whooping. Armitage was grim. Crosston, despite his bravado, could scarcely hide his fright.

Ten Pennies spoke: "Fight."

Neither moved. The half-breed walked to his horse and there found a long whip. Returning, he lashed the shoulders of Armitage, leaving a long bloody gash.

"Fight!"

"No."

The lash came down again. Armitage bit his lip, but did not cry out.

"We have no choice," Crosston said. He gave a tentative wave of his knife.

"We had one," Armitage said. "This was your idea, not theirs."

"And it was your idea to pry into affairs that didn't concern you," Crosston said. "I cannot afford to leave you alive."

Armitage stood and looked at his blade, still unwilling. But Crosston swung at him again, almost cutting him a second time.

This time, Armitage slashed back.

Caine dismounted at the foot of a slope and tethered his horse. With rifle in hand he climbed, gritting his teeth against the pain of it, until at last he topped a high ridge looking across a narrow valley.

They were there, below. The renegades gathered in a circle. Caine heard their shouts and laughter. Armitage and Crosston were fighting, slashing at each other with blades. There was blood on Armitage's back and chest.

Caine lay on his belly and sighted down the rifle, putting the bead on Ten Pennies' head. His finger began a slow squeeze on the trigger.

There was a sudden thud. Something like fire shot across Caine's vision, and he went numb. The rifle dropped, his eyes fluttered, and he fell unconscious.

"Kill him now, Brannigan?" queried Artemus Frye.

"No. I want him alive for a while. Look yonder, Art. What a fight, huh?"

The renegades became frenzied, thrilled by the new vigor of the combatants. For his part, Armitage was raging mad that Crosston, a man he once had trusted, even liked, was trying to kill him.

Armitage finally understood Crosston, as he pivoted and jabbed with his knife. Crosston cared only about one thing—recovering his treasure hidden to the north. Nothing else mattered, not promises, not the life of any other man. It was clear now, but the realization came too late.

It was neat and convenient, Armitage had to admit. Fear of Sam Ten Pennies was the sole reason Crosston had hired him and Caine to begin with. By winning this fight, Crosston could obtain the safe passage he had sought all along. He would no longer need either of them.

The older man slashed at Crosston and noted how tired he was beginning to feel.

Crosston lunged and thrust his knife into Armitage's shoulder. The other grunted and pulled away, jerking the blade free as he did so. Blood streamed down to the pounded dirt at his feet.

The old Civil War veteran snarled and swung his knife in a wide arc. Crosston gave out a shrill scream and pulled back. Blood ran down his hand. His little finger was nearly sliced off.

"Let's make a run," Armitage said as best his strained lungs would let him. "Let's try to live."

"I intend to live," Crosston responded.

His knife sang through air and drew blood once more, bringing a loud cheer from the renegades. Ten Pennies alone showed no emotion—he merely observed.

Armitage jerked suddenly on the cord binding him to Crosston, unbalancing the Englishman. His knife came down as Crosston slid past him like a bull swiping a matador, but it inflicted only a minor cut to Crosston's bicep.

The younger man pivoted and slashed, barely missing Armitage's gut. The latter jerked the cord again, but this time Crosston was ready. He jerked back simultaneously, and it was Armitage who stumbled. Crosston's knife came down and plunged deep into the older man's back.

"*Simon!*" The name burst from Armitage instinctively.

He was terribly weak now, and hurting. He bled profusely, and Crosston's image wavered before him like a heat demon. He poked with his blade and nicked Crosston's arm, but his fight was gone. Armitage realized his hope for survival was gone too.

He dropped his knife and slumped forward. Crosston moved in and put his blade through his opponent's heart.

17

Caine came to and found himself tied to a sapling. His head throbbed like a hammer-struck anvil. About twenty feet away Brannigan and Frye sat eating jerky and crackers. Brannigan smiled broadly at him.

"Howdy, Simon Caine!" he said. "Pleased to make your acquaintance. My name's Cordell Brannigan. You've never met me. You met my brother in Henley, though. You recall him?"

"Where is Jake?" Caine said. His throat was scratchy and his voice was like a rasp against wood.

"Was he fighting in the Indian camp?"

"Yes."

"Well, the old one's dead as a rock. The boy stuck him."

Caine leaned to one side and was sick.

"They turned the boy loose when it was done. Even give him a horse. We watched it all from the ridge, me and Artemus, here. Artemus Frye."

"Good to meet you, Caine," Frye said around a mouthful of cracker.

"Artemus here will be the one to end your earthly existence once we get near Henley," Brannigan said. "He's partial to his machete, and besides, we'll have to prove to Montrose that we really got you. Your head will do real fine."

"Are you sure the older one was dead?" Caine asked.

"Deader than John Quincy Adams's great-grandma. He was a friend of yours, huh? Bet you'd like to get your hands on the boy what killed him. He the Englisher who busted you out of jail?"

Caine, his head in his hands, did not answer.

"What were you doing here, anyway?" Brannigan asked.

Caine, too numbed to do anything else, answered truthfully. "Looking for a treasure."

The broad, mirthful face went serious. "What?"

Caine said, "You heard me."

Brannigan gave an uncertain chuckle. "Say now, you wouldn't josh an old boy, would you?"

Caine looked up through bleary eyes. "What you are I don't josh with. I smear it under my foot."

Brannigan's eye twitched at the insult, but Caine had caught his attention. Brannigan rose and came over to him. "What kind of treasure?"

Caine hesitated only a second, then: "I don't know."

Brannigan leaned down in Caine's face. Frye joined him. "You don't know?"

Caine spat on them.

Frye cursed and gripped his machete, but Brannigan caught his arm. "Easy, Frye. Maybe he's telling the truth." He turned back to Caine. "You know where it is?"

"I know."

"You know *what* it is too—you just ain't telling."

"I told you, I don't know."

"You'll tell me. You'll sing it like a choir boy." To Frye he said: "Artemus, we got a new hand to play here. We let Montrose wait a little longer, let Caine

107

lead us to this treasure, if there is one. He gets us to it, we just might let him go. He don't, and we head back to Montrose, just like we planned. Nothing lost but a little time at the worst."

"What if he gets loose?" Frye countered. "Sounds to me like he's trying to save his hide."

"If he's lying, we'll find out soon enough. And he won't get loose. We'll keep him in such a shape that if he does, he won't be able to get nowhere."

Brannigan addressed Caine: "Looks like you got a chance to live, outlaw. Do what we tell you, and you'll be fine. If not, you're a dead man. But first you talk." Brannigan punctuated his demand with a hard slap across Caine's jaw.

Caine relaxed to ease the sting of the blow, but he had to struggle to retain his consciousness, for his head still ached as if squeezed in a vise.

"Only the boy knew what the treasure was," Caine said. "He never told us."

Brannigan drew back his hand, then dropped it. Muttering, he moved away and talked covertly to Frye. He came back and wordlessly cut Caine's bonds.

They lashed Caine to the horn of Brannigan's saddle, using a long rope. Packs were set and guns checked, and Brannigan and Frye mounted.

"You walk out front. Head for that treasure. You fall, and I'll drag you. I get a notion you're leading us to nothing, and I'll drop you where you stand. You understand me?"

"I need water," Caine said.

The answer was a jerk on the rope. Caine staggered forward, dizzy and sick. He blinked and shook his head, trying to clear his vision.

He walked a long time, heading north. He thought

about John Crosston. Where the treasure was, there Crosston would go. Caine knew generally where that would be, for he had seen Crosston's map a few times at the outset of their venture. In a cavern overlooking Ten Pennies' valley. But which cavern? Could he find it?

The sun grew hot as they traveled. Brannigan was relentless, pushing him on like a mule.

Caine concentrated on the trail, on Crosston, on the treasure. One thing he had to confess to himself: all the subtle points Crosston had made about the treasure made sense now that Caine knew what it supposedly was. No wonder Crosston had been willing to pay such a high price for protection.

The money. Crosston had paid him five thousand dollars, a sizable wad of bills Caine had kept in his trouser pocket. But now it was gone, and that was a puzzlement. Brannigan didn't seem the kind of man to find such a sum and not crow about it. Yet he had said nothing.

That could mean two things: either Brannigan had taken the cash and was trying to hide it from Frye, or Frye had taken it and was trying to hide it from Brannigan.

On they plodded, Caine losing track of the hours, Frye intoning an old hymn somewhere behind him. His head pounded to the staggering of his feet.

The day wore on. Since this morning Caine had been given nothing to eat or drink. When darkness fell, though, they made a camp and Brannigan offered him water. Caine drank it lustily.

He was surprised when Brannigan built a fire.

"You ain't much worried about Ten Pennies, are you?" he said.

"That the 'breed? I ain't afraid of him," Brannigan

said. He had been sipping occasionally from a bottle all day, and was sufficiently intoxicated to throw aside caution.

Frye was busy sharpening his machete. The long black blade threw back the firelight. "I understand, Caine, you have a brother who is a preacher," he said.

Caine looked at the darkening sky, silent.

"What does he think about the life you lead?"

"Not your affair."

"Doesn't like it too much, I would suppose."

Brannigan laughed. "Get used to it, Caine. Frye's getting ready for one of his religious talks. He knows that Bible from Genesis to Revelations."

Eerily, Frye moved to where Caine was tied and touched the tip of the machete to Caine's hand.

"The hand of a gunman," he said. "A hand that has killed many men. 'If thy right hand offend thee, cut it off.' What do you think, Caine? Would you like to be free of the killing hand? 'Without the shedding of blood there is no remission of sins.' Better to enter heaven without a hand than hell with all your limbs. Shall I free you of your killing hand, Caine?"

Caine stared into the crazed face, unspeaking.

"Leave him be, Artemus," Brannigan said. "Your time is coming—unless Caine is really telling the truth about that treasure."

"I don't believe he is. I believe he's leading us up the path."

"Speaking of treasure," Caine said, "how did you divide my five thousand dollars?"

Brannigan looked up sharply. "What five thousand?" Frye's features stiffened, his lip curling back a half second in a snarl worthy of a beaten cur.

"Paper money, right in my pocket," Caine said. "You must have taken it."

"What do you know about this, Frye?" demanded Brannigan.

"Nothing. He's lying again."

"Is he?"

"'Course he is. I don't know nothing about no money."

Brannigan started to say something else, but didn't. He sat back and relaxed. "Reckon you just dropped it somewhere, Caine. Too bad. I've killed men for less bounty than that. Whole lot less."

They roasted a rabbit and gave Caine a little. Not nearly enough, but a little.

That night Caine slept without dreams.

He awoke to the smell of coffee, sunlight in his face. Brannigan was pouring two steaming cupfuls. He brought one to Caine. The outlaw accepted it, cupping it between his bound hands.

Brannigan was actually jovial.

"A little accident last night, I'm sorry to say," he said. "I can't imagine how it happened."

Caine looked at Frye's bedroll. The man was on his back, eyes tightly shut. His machete was thrust through his chest and into the ground.

Brannigan walked away, whistling. He patted his bulging pocket in time to the tune.

18

Time for Caine slid by in hours of heat and exhaustion, thirst and hunger, and pain from the scab-clotted wound on his head. Moving ever northward, they at last penetrated the valley of Sam Ten Pennies.

Caine struggled to remember the details of the map Crosston had shown him. Though uncertain, he never faltered, for to do so would have invited a bullet from Brannigan.

The valley was vast, wide, and green up to the timberline. They traveled through it several hours, Caine heading for a ridge where he knew there were caverns similar to those marked on Crosston's map. Darkness came and he passed another night of death-like sleep. The morning broke and they moved again in the same monotonous way.

As they moved up along broken land, Caine found the tracks of an unshod horse. Later, where a jumbling of the tracks indicated the horse's rider had dismounted to let the beast graze, Caine found boot prints, small English boots like Crosston's. He knew then he was near the mark.

The tracks were old, though. And later he found fresher ones heading the opposite direction. Either Crosston had gotten lost and doubled back or had found his treasure and begun his return home.

Caine said nothing of this to Brannigan, for it would not do for the bounty hunter to believe the treasure was removed. Brannigan himself never noted the tracks, for he was always drinking, throwing aside both caution and attention. Caine silently observed his captor's behavior and waited for his chance.

As they moved up a narrow ravine that broadened to a rocky slope, the bounty hunter dismounted because of the steepness and trudged heavily along behind Caine. They climbed until the valley was far below, and then Caine made his move.

Near the top of the slope he pivoted, leaping down toward Brannigan. His foot pounded into the soft pillow of the fat man's belly. Wind bursting from his lungs, Brannigan tilted back and rolled down the long slope in a jumble of dust and bruises.

Frye's blood-caked machete, kept by Brannigan as a souvenir, was keen and made quick work of Caine's bonds. He was free even before Brannigan had stopped rolling.

Brannigan had slung Caine's Spencer and his gunbelt to his saddlehorn, and now Caine loosened them, along with a cloth sack full of ammunition, as Brannigan staggered to his feet at the base of the slope. There was no time for Caine to load.

Brannigan had lost his rifle as he rolled, but his pistol was secure in its holster, held by a leather thong. He drew the weapon and fired at the outlaw.

The shot sang high past Caine, but spooked the horses. They angled down the slope and vanished into the woodlands.

Caine scrambled upward and cut across a bare rock face. He topped the crest of the slope, then turned left and darted through a conifer grove. A few yards beyond he found a dry streambed that led farther into the forest.

More rocks ahead; he ran for them. Risking exposure for a moment, he climbed over the face of a massive boulder, then found his way back into the forest. Dodging along an uneven path, he ran where the ground was rocky and would leave no tracks. Coming to more broken land, he darted among boulders and rock slabs. Then, head throbbing, he dropped to the earth beside a small stream, immersed his face in it and drank.

He splashed water through his beard and across his face and slowly raised himself. Then he saw a track.

It was the biggest he had ever seen, longer by a good three or four inches than the average man's foot. Whoever made it wore moccasins, the depth of the track indicating he was quite heavy.

Caine stared at it, amazed, then through his mind flashed words spoken by John Crosston at the beginning of the journey, and other words written in the journal.

"So you didn't die after all," Caine muttered.

He rested a long time, until he was sure Brannigan was not near. Then he stood and began following the tracks, curious and eager to see if at the end of the trail he would find Crosston's treasure, and maybe Crosston himself.

He doubted he would. The hoofmarks he had seen suggested Crosston had come and gone. Then again, if the treasure's keeper was about, maybe Crosston would not have been able to get past him. Especially if he was as big as these tracks indicated.

But knowing well how far the young Englishman was willing to go, Caine was unsure that even a man as big as this one could keep Crosston back. Jake had paid the price for Crosston's zealotry, as had a priest back in Boston, according to the scribblings in Crosston's journal.

Caine moved on, following the massive footprints.

Meanwhile, Brannigan also was moving, cursing with every step. Caine was gone, and the bounty hunter had not even a horse to carry him out of these mountains. At least he still had his weapons.

Brannigan scanned the Bitterroot land around him, keeping watch for Caine as well as the half-breed Caine had called Ten Pennies. Thinking about it, Brannigan recalled some dime-novel folklore about such a half-breed. He supposedly was a particularly vicious hater of whites. Now that he was alone in these mountains for the first time, Brannigan felt a shiver of fear. He thanked the heavens for his rifle and sidearm.

For nearly an hour he followed the curve of the valley, until it gave way to hills, then to rocky country. Brannigan had hoped to encounter a stream by now, but so far, no luck. No sign of the lost horses, either.

He climbed a slope because the land's contours left him no choice. It was for the best, anyway; from high up he could gain a good vantage point of the whole valley.

He went on until he could go no farther. He sat down in the shade of a juniper and let his pounding heart calm itself. The shade was cool. He closed his eyes.

When he opened them, some time had passed. He stiffened, for below he saw the lost horses. But the half-breed and his band were there too.

They did not see him yet. He sat there, ludicrously

exposed, watching the renegades examining the horses and pilfering the saddlebags and pack.

They mounted and rode away, taking the horses. Brannigan closed his eyes and exhaled.

He headed farther up. At the top of the ridge he was exhausted and desperately thirsty, but heard running water not far away. Following his ears, he headed down the other side of the ridge, until at last he saw a stream running out of the mountainside. It flowed from a sizable cavern. He ran to it and drank. When he had finished, he stood and looked directly into the cave. All was blackness, enclosed and dank. Brannigan feared nothing more than darkness and enclosure. He turned away.

He heard the horses before they came into view, and that saved him. Ten Pennies again. He and his band had doubled back around the ridge and come up the other side. Brannigan wondered for a panicked moment if they were after him. Then he saw that the dirt at his feet was trampled flat. He had stumbled upon one of Ten Pennies' watering holes.

The only escape route was into the cave. Brannigan entered and picked his way along in darkness. He thought about stopping and holding still until Ten Pennies was gone, but the oppressive cave and his fear of the half-breed kept him moving. He could not bear to be still in this darkness. Besides, if he followed the stream, he couldn't get lost. Deeper he went.

Some time later he realized his feet were scrunching on dirt and gravel rather than splashing water. The stream was gone. No water at his heels, just bare rock.

He moved within the span of a few feet. Nothing.

He had wandered out of the stream and now he couldn't find it.

Someday somebody going to hurt you. Someday somebody'll put you down in a hole, like you done my kitty! The voice of Henry Cleek came clearly to him.

"Get hold of yourself, old boy." The sound of a human voice, even his own, was comforting, so he said it again. "Get hold of yourself, old boy."

He stood, breathing deeply, clutching the stock of his rifle. Deliberately, carefully, he moved forward, feeling his way along.

Though he tried to remain calm, despair was overcoming him. It would have been best to have hidden just inside the cave's mouth until Ten Pennies was gone. Too late now. He sank to the floor and longed for sunlight and space.

Then, against the background of pure night, he saw a spot of lightness. Not really light, just lightness. It was so dim he thought it might be an illusion.

Keeping his eyes on it, he stood again and crept forward. He ignored the abrasions of the rocks against him. The farther he traveled, the more sure he was—the lightness was really there, and becoming brighter.

It was an opening, a downward hole at his feet. Below he could discern only more rock, but the light had to come from some outside opening nearby. He sat on the hole's brink and let his feet dangle in, then hesitated. What if his eyes were fooling him? How far down were those rocks? The idea of falling into the heart of a mountain was too horrible to consider.

His gun. He could drop it and see how long it fell. He did, and the rifle clattered against stone only a few feet below.

Brannigan slid through and dropped in a heap at the base of the passage.

The light came from behind him. Picking up his rifle, he moved toward it. It grew brighter. A gust of fresh air struck him deliciously, and he almost cried.

Here the cavern widened and the light was bright enough to illuminate the walls. He rounded a bend in the passage and stopped, frowning and looking around him.

"What kind of place is this?"

On the floor of the cave lay furs, cast about in a seemingly random way, along with assorted trash, bones, ragged pelts, handmade tools, flints, and wood stacked beside a heap of black ash where repeated fires had been built. Smoke residue was thick on the walls.

He slowly stepped through. He caught a glimpse of something, someone, against a wall.

He raised his rifle, then saw it was not a man who looked back at him.

It had been a man once, but now it was only a skeleton, crumbling, dressed in a parchment-dry bearskin robe that hung on it, a decayed shroud.

Brannigan looked more closely. He noticed the curving of the fingers, cupped together on the lap, but holding only empty air.

He remembered Caine's treasure story and wondered, but discounted it. The outlaw probably made it up to save himself. He was a fool to have listened.

The lure of treasure gone, the memory of being lost in the darkness shadowing him, Brannigan wanted nothing but to be free of enclosing walls.

He blinked in the afternoon light as he emerged. Scanning the landscape, he looked for evidence of human presence and found none. Then his eyes dropped to his feet and grew wide.

"God a'mighty! Like a bear in moccasins!"

The entire area fronting the cave was trampled and marked with huge tracks. Bigger even than Brannigan's own large feet. He cocked his head and frowned. Nobody was *this* big.

Finally he found a recess in a hillside and slid behind a tangle of brush. His hand slid to his pocket, and he realized suddenly he had lost his roll of bills. Funny—after being lost in that cave, it hardly seemed to matter.

He lay down and quickly fell asleep.

19

Caine stood at the mouth of the cave, rifle ready. The tracks had led him here, and now, mingled among them, he saw more sign that John Crosston had been here before him. The treasure, probably, was in his hands.

If the treasure really was what the journal said, there was something wrong about Crosston having it. It was like a rat with a jewel in its mouth. Crosston wasn't worthy of it.

No more unworthy than me. Caine resisted the idea. *Everything I've done has been for the sake of justice.* But the thought had a hollow ring.

Caine looked into the cavern. If the occupant of this cavern had resisted Crosston, Crosston might have shot him. If so, he would likely be inside somewhere, dead or hurt.

Caine stepped into the darkness, waited for his eyes to adjust, then went forward. He could hear his own heartbeat. The air was close and tight.

When he found the skeleton, he stood before it a long time, looking into the eye sockets.

"Hello, thief," he said. He glanced at the cupped, empty hands. "You kept watch over it a long time, old man."

He walked on until the darkness was too dense for him to see. He lit a match, and as the yellow flare burst, he caught a whiff of decay. Something dead.

He looked about, expecting to find the body of the one who had left the tracks. What was the name written in Crosston's journal? Gideon, he recalled.

But Caine found no body. A heap of animal carcasses was the source of the stench. It appeared to be composed largely of ground squirrels and rabbits—even a few hawks and a buzzard. They were just bone and ragged meat, as if they had been gnawed raw and tossed aside. The match fizzled out.

Deeper in the cave, unseen, a hulking form shifted in the darkness, a whisper of movement Caine could not be sure he had heard. He quickly struck another match and peered about. All was still. He saw strings of something hanging from a crude rack of sticks near the cave wall. He touched it. Dried venison.

He turned back toward the cave entrance. He felt something, invisible and unheard, looked back again into the blackness, but couldn't see anything.

He emerged into sunlight.

"Caine!"

The voice came from somewhere close beside him. He wheeled.

It was Brannigan. "Right good to see you again, Simon Caine! You just hold still while I scramble your brain like an egg."

He was shapeless against the sun, with his rifle raised and aimed squarely at him. "Drop your rifle," he said, and Caine did. "You'd best pray if you know how," the bounty hunter said. "This time I'm taking no chances. It ends here."

As Brannigan spoke, Caine edged backward and

around. Brannigan moved with him step for step. Caine slid his hand to his gunbelt.

"Don't think about it!" Brannigan stepped in front of the cave. "Your time has come, Caine." He sighted down the barrel, squinting.

For a second Caine imagined it was a piece of night that emerged from the cavern and engulfed the bounty hunter. The creature that took Brannigan in its grasp was nearly seven feet tall, a Goliath of a man.

He dwarfed Brannigan as he wrapped his arms around the bounty hunter's chest. He squeezed until Brannigan's eyes rolled up in their sockets. The giant then tossed the body aside; it rolled down the slope into brush, the rifle rattling down after it.

The mountain on legs turned to Caine.

The outlaw responded reflexively. He drew his pistol and fired a shot into the fur-clad bulk before him.

He saw the eyes as the bullet struck. They were as childish as those of his son, staring up at him from a trundle bed on the banks of the Calfkiller River.

Gideon turned, whimpering, and ran back into the cavern. Caine dropped his pistol, squeezed shut his eyes, and in an instant he understood the truth that his nightmares had been trying to convey to him for so many nights now, and knew also from where it came.

It came from himself—or himself as he would have been if he had left vengeance to the heavens those long years back. It was simple: *There must be an end.*

He looked into the cavern, thinking all the wrongs he had done seemed small compared to what had just happened. He had shot Gideon simply because it had become his way to hurt and kill. Suddenly it seemed absurd.

Caine entered the cave and searched for the one he had shot. He did not find him. He searched also for Brannigan, and—strangely—could not find him either. He returned to the cavern mouth and sat alone until sunset reddened the sky and darkness followed.

Sam Ten Pennies also sat alone, his head buried in his hands. The malady that ate away his sanity had caused his band to abandon him at last.

He lifted his face when he heard someone approaching. His mental illness robbed him of perception, so he saw not the face of Opequon, but that of his slain mate. He extended his arms, welcoming the miracle without question.

Opequon stopped. She moved as if to raise Jack Whitaker's old Hawken rifle, but did not. Finally she turned and walked away.

This was the one abandonment Sam Ten Pennies could not endure. He rose and followed her, but she moved swiftly and with elusive skill that kept her always a flitting, distant ghost. Finally he lost sight of her.

He ran to the top of a ridge and looked across his valley. He shouted her name and the echo called back, but she did not.

When the sun grew hot, he ceased calling and sat down. He leaned against a boulder and waited, but she did not come. When night fell again, still he waited, and on through the next day and night, until many weeks later the renegades who had abandoned him found his body slumped against the rock, his dead eyes still gazing across the valley.

Ezra Cleek did not know what had made him awaken. He sat upright and saw a tall figure standing beside his bed. He drew in his breath. A cold voice said to him: "I want a horse."

He recognized the voice as Simon Caine's. The old man's heart pounded.

"I— What are you—"

"Don't sit there stammering. Get me a horse."

Cleek nodded. He rose, trembling, and pulled dirty clothing over his even dirtier body. Caine remained beside him, face hidden in the darkness, and that made him seem particularly threatening.

But even frightened, Ezra Cleek was a businessman. He said, "I've got nothing very good right now, so your price will be low—"

"You're going to give it to me," Caine said.

Cleek chewed his tongue. "Yes. Of course."

He walked, stooped from the stiffness of his aging bones, out to the horse pen. Caine followed. The tall Confederate studied the handful of horses and pointed to one.

"A good choice, Mr. Caine," Cleek said. He opened the pen and fetched the animal. "Enjoy him."

"A saddle."

"A saddle. Yes." Cleek shuffled off to a shed and came back, puffing beneath the weight of an old saddle. Caine took it, threw it across the horse, and cinched it.

When he looked at Cleek again, the old man was pointing a derringer into his face and smiling.

"It appears I've got you, Mr. Caine."

Caine walked to him, wrenched away the derringer, and grasped Cleek by the neck in one steeltrap hand. He pulled the little man up to his tiptoes and drew his face to his own.

"I'd snap your scrawny neck except for one reason, and he's sleeping in your station yonder. God knows he deserves better than what he's got for a pa, but I'll not rob him of what little he has." He shoved Cleek to the ground, mounted, and rode away.

Later that night, another man came to Cleek's Station, and this time it was Henry Cleek who heard him, or, at least, sensed his presence. The young man rose, picked up the kitten that slept beside him, slid out his window and looked about in the moonlight.

He saw the man approaching. He was amazingly big, like a huge shadow in the moonlight. Silently he came to Henry Cleek and stopped.

For several moments the two looked at each other. Then Henry Cleek smiled and held up his kitten.

20

Helena, Montana Territory

Deputy Jim Ballentree, newest member of the staff of the town marshal of Helena, stood in the afternoon sunshine, cutting a long chew of tobacco from a plug and pondering his own happiness. A long-skirted woman passed him with a rustle and teasing scent of perfume, and he tipped his hat. He settled the chew into his jaw and walked slowly down the boardwalk. It was a daily afternoon ritual for him now, one he liked. There wasn't much about this job he didn't like, except the low pay. It was a world away from Henley, and he was satisfied.

His wife also seemed happier here. Ballentree had realized now that the days in Henley had been hard ones for her. She, more than himself, had sensed the oppressive shadow of William Montrose on the town. Ballentree had feigned a lot of independence in those days, but he never really had been free to be the kind of marshal he wanted to be.

Ballentree leaned over, spat a dollop of tobacco, adjusted his hat and turned the corner. The building that marked the end of his daily rounds was the Montana House, a three-story hotel with its own dining room and stable, plus an authentic Chinaman to pour water over you in your own ten-cents-per-half-hour enameled bathtub. It was a popular hotel, and its owner, Benjamin Landers, was a well-off man.

Ballentree liked Landers, who was a few years older than he. Landers had taken on the task of making the new deputy feel welcome, and the pair enjoyed their daily conversations at the end of Ballentree's rounds. It was usually no more than a two-minute exchange, after which Ballentree returned to the office to do the standard least-seniority job of paperwork. Indeed, this task was the symbolic end of the day for him, for it was immediately followed by the ride home to his wife and the aroma of the waiting supper.

Ballentree entered the Montana House lobby and removed his hat. Delicious smells wafted across from the dining room, putting him in mind again of the supper he anticipated. The lobby was a beautiful work of architecture and craftsmanship, by western standards: fine mahogany paneling, imported from Chicago; fancy brass lamps, all enveloped in a burnished-gold atmosphere enhanced by sunlight through the west-facing windowpanes.

Ben Landers stood behind the lobby desk, his thumbs hooked in his vest pockets. "Afternoon, Jim."

"Ben."

"All well with you?" It was his standard afternoon query.

"Fine."

They went through their usual banter, then Landers surprised Ballentree with a supper invitation for three nights hence. He accepted, agreeing with the hotel owner that the visit would give their wives a chance to meet and maybe strike a friendship.

A young black man stepped out of the dining room, balancing a tray covered in a checked cloth. He swept up the stairs in straight-spined dignity, wearing the red velvet jacket Landers required of all his employees.

Ballentree watched the waiter disappear around the landing. Landers, having just lighted a cigar, waved his smoking matchstick toward the stairs.

"Funny thing," he said. "We have us a hermit of sorts living here. He's been here nearly three weeks, and he's stayed in his room since he arrived. He walked in one day, rented out a room for a night, and picked up a letter that was waiting for him. He took it upstairs, and since then he's been a fixture. He rented out his room a month ahead and started taking his meals up there, and he's ordered God knows how many bottles of whiskey. He never comes out. Must slip out in the night to empty his chamber pot. He signed in as Williamson."

Ballentree said, "Has he given you any trouble?"

"No. He just stays up there, all alone."

"Figure he's waiting on someone?"

"If he is, he's never said." He paused, then spoke more solemnly: "You know, it's crossed my mind that we'll find him up there some morning, dead."

"You want me to check him out?"

Landers considered, then shook his head. "Not just yet."

"Just let me know, then. Williamson, you say?"

"Yes."

"I'll check our records and see if he might be wanted. What was the first name?"

"John, I believe."

"John Williamson. I'll see what I can turn up. But for now I'd best be going."

"Good evening. Don't forget that supper date."

"I won't." Ballentree slipped on his hat and headed for the door.

"Jim."

"Yeah?" He turned back to Landers.

"He's not American. Sounded British to me."

Ballentree hesitated for a second and then continued out onto the porch. On the horizon clouds had gathered and thunder rumbled. Just like that night in Henley, he thought. Feeling disconcerted, he headed for the office to flip through wanted posters.

Gideon's pain grew worse with every step. He had been able to overcome it so far, and keep his head, but now he was beginning to despair.

His struggle to keep up with the tall man who he had followed from the cavern had been difficult from the beginning. Gideon had managed to do it as long as the man was on foot. But when the man had gotten a horse, Gideon lost him. Now he had reached a place where windows glowed here and there on the mountainsides at night and there were cattle and roads and people.

He was hungry; here he found less of the roots and berries and animal flesh left by the mountain carrion birds that had sustained him—barely—up until now.

He was bleeding again, too, and the wounds, when he dared look at them, were horrible to see. So he made himself not look at them, and concentrated on his mission.

He prayed for guidance, though without words. Unhearing, Gideon had never learned to speak. But as best he could, his father had taught him of the thing they guarded, their duty toward it—Gideon's duty alone, now—and of the God they served in fulfilling that duty.

Below Gideon lay a valley. He saw lights. There was a house, a barn, fences, and a chicken coop with hens and roosters scratching around it in the twilight. He recognized none of these things as such, but knew the birds would be food.

Breathing heavily, Gideon stumbled into the valley as night descended.

Old Bailey, they called him. First name, last name—which it was, nobody knew or cared, least of all Bailey himself. Too many years washed away by whiskey had wiped out all such trivialities.

Bailey was on hard times at the moment. No money, no liquor, and nobody needing a saloon swept or a stable shoveled clean. He hadn't had a drop since last night, and had been shaky all day. He huddled against a shed wall on a side street, knees pulled against his chest and his arms wrapped around his calves. It was dark, a storm was blowing up, and he was cold. But the need for a drink was all that really concerned him.

He heard a noise and looked up to see a rider gazing down at him. "Hello," the stranger said.

"'Lo."

"Where could a man find a hotel in this town?"

"You want good or cheap?"

"Good. The ones a man would go to if he had money and was used to spending it."

Old Bailey thought it through. "The Montana House is where I'd go if I was such a man. I ain't, though. I'm just a broke old drunk who they wouldn't let in the back door."

Simon Caine studied the old man silently. He dug

a hand into his pocket and produced a greenback, the one bill the bounty hunters had not found when they robbed him. He let it flutter to the ground. "Thanks, old man," he said.

Old Bailey watched him go, then picked up the bill. A ten-dollar note. He stared at it, disbelieving, then kissed it. He looked up at the cloud-roiled sky.

The rider must have been an angel, straight from heaven's gate.

21

The Montana House lobby was empty except for Landers' cleaning boy when Simon Caine entered. The boy stared blank-eyed at him, then went back to sweeping. Caine walked up the stairs.

He reached the second level, turned down the hallway and stopped. He believed Crosston was here, somewhere, but he had no proof, and no idea which room he would be in. He thought of asking the cleaning boy, but with the purpose he had in mind, such advertising might be unwise.

Caine leaned against a wall, thinking about what to do. Why had he been forced to argue with himself all the way here from the Bitterroots, firming his conviction by day and watching it dissolve at sunset?

A door opened and closed. A man in a derby fumbled with his key three doors down. When he finished and came toward Caine, the outlaw touched his arm. The man stopped.

"I'm looking for a young Englishman. You know what room he'd be in?"

"Did you ask at the desk?"

"No one there."

"Well, I heard there was a foreign man in 312. I don't know if he's English."

"Obliged." He let the man go, and climbed to the next level.

At the door of room 312 he stood in silence. At his feet was a tray of dirty dishes still scrapped with fragments. He raised his fist, hesitated again, then knocked.

"Just take the tray," came a voice from inside. It was Crosston's, but it was different than he remembered it.

Caine tried the latch. It was locked. He stepped back and kicked open the door.

Crosston lay on the bed. He was unshaven, his hair matted and dark with sweat. The clothes he wore obviously had not been changed in weeks. The stench of stale liquor permeated the room, which was lit by two lamps, one attached to the wall and another on the night table beside Crosston.

The young Englishman barely reacted to the crashing of the door. He turned bleary eyes toward Caine, showing neither surprise nor fear. Caine had seen the same look in the faces of mortally wounded soldiers on bloodied battlefields.

For a time neither man spoke. Then Crosston pushed himself up on one elbow and said, "Hello, Caine. Pardon me if I don't get up, but I'm very drunk." He looked away, toward the dresser across from the foot of the bed.

"Well, there it is. That's what I've spent years searching for, what I broke you out of jail for, what I've killed for. It's beautiful in a rather simple way, eh?"

Caine's gaze followed Crosston's to the dresser.

A chalice stood there, shining in the dull light of the lamps. It was wide at the flange, tapered toward a round base, and appeared to be made of bronze. It was unembellished. Just a plain chalice, apparently very old.

"Do you know, Caine, why a man would do all I have for such a meager thing as that?"

Caine said, "I read your journal in the cabin. I know what it is."

"Ah, do you? No, Caine, you don't. No more than I did."

Caine did not understand the remark, and did not respond. But something from Crosston's journal came to his mind, and he said: "Carried by Joseph of—"

Crosston nodded and cut in: "Joseph of Arimathea. Brought by him to Britain, then by the Magdalen to Marseilles. From there it has traveled far, possessed at various times by Knights Templar, Albigensian heretics, by the Church itself. It has been stolen and traded and smuggled and sold, and the men I killed were not the first to die because of it. So goes the story of the long-sought Holy Grail." He paused, then sadly continued: "But as it pertains to the chalice you see there, a story is all it is."

"What do you mean?"

"It's a fraud. A lie. If the Grail survives today, as I believe it does, that is not it."

"How do you know?"

Crosston reached to the table beside his bed and picked up a crumpled letter. He tossed it toward Caine; it drifted down to his feet.

"From my father. I had told him he could reach me here when all this was done, and I gave him the name I would use. What that letter tells me is that all these years of searching have been a waste. My father was duped. The broker who sold the cup to him was a swindler. He played on my father's obsession, knew enough facts to convince him the cup really was the Grail. My father now knows the truth about him. And about the cup. The years and devotion he spent, the money and the danger—just to be duped by a swindler."

"I don't give a damn about your father," Caine said. "Are you telling me that Jake died for absolutely nothing at all?"

Crosston laughed bitterly. "So he did. Isn't that irony for you, Caine? But Jake wasn't the only one. I killed a priest because of that cup. I felt I had to. Somehow he learned the location of it; he might have reached it before me. Funny. He was swindled too. Probably by the same man who cheated my father."

Caine drew his pistol and aimed it at Crosston. The Englishman smiled faintly. "So you're going to kill me? I don't really care, you know. My father is all in this world that has ever mattered to me. More than anything, I wanted to do something important for him, something to show him how much— But it doesn't matter. I've failed. Kill me, if you've got to. If you don't, I'll probably just do it myself."

Caine sighted down the barrel and clicked back the hammer.

Gideon ran from the farmstead, frightened by the hot flare of a shotgun blast that had fanned his head. Even though he wasn't hit, his clumsy efforts to save himself had further torn his previous wounds.

He went far and fell to the ground. He was lost, badly hurt, and was beginning to fear he would never see his treasure again. He would, instead, die here alone, far from his cavern and the presence of his father.

Being alone did not frighten him, but this distance

from all he knew, and the separation from the sole item of importance in his life, was unbearable.

The thunder crashed again, and rain came down at bullet speed, driving into the earth and his skin. At length he arose, strength almost gone, and began wandering randomly.

22

Jim Ballentree stood, knocking over his chair. He read the paper in his hand again, speaking the key parts: "Ian John Crosston . . . England . . . murder of priest . . . speaks with noticeable accent . . ."

He folded and pocketed the notice. He slid on his hat, drew his pistol and checked the loads, then left the office. He walked fast through the darkness, heading for the Montana House, splashing puddles and smelling the pungency of the just-passed storm.

Inside he climbed the stairs and moved stealthily down the dark hallways, hardly breathing, listening to silence. He rested his right hand on the butt of his pistol. Curse his pounding heart—the Englishman would hear it, it beat so loudly.

Up the hallway he saw a door ajar. He slid forward. The door was open just a few inches. The lock was shattered, as if kicked in.

Something at his feet drew his attention. A dark line was running from beneath the door and across the hall. Ballentree knelt and touched it. It was blood.

Ballentree drew his pistol and pushed open the door. Warily he looked inside.

On the bed lay the Englishman he had encountered in Henley. His face was pale and his eyes half closed. His left arm dangled over the side of the bed, a long, ragged cut gaping open from wrist to elbow. Blood drained from it in a thinning stream, pouring into and overflowing a shallow metal cup into which the fingers dangled. Beside the cup lay a bloodied piece of a broken bottle.

Ballentree holstered his pistol and rushed to the bed. He raised the bleeding arm. Crosston's dull gaze lifted to him and the coated lips moved slightly.

Ballentree pulled a handkerchief from his pocket and knotted it around the slashed arm. The flow of blood diminished, then stopped.

Crosston's lips moved again, whispering words Ballentree could not hear.

"Why did you do it?" Ballentree asked, expecting no answer.

But John Crosston's good arm came up and he weakly grasped Ballentree's wrist. He spoke with effort, and this time Ballentree understood: "He didn't kill me."

"Who?"

"Simon Caine."

Crosston's eyes closed and his lips parted. He fell unconscious, leaving Ballentree wondering if he had heard correctly.

"Did you say Simon Caine?"

Crosston could not answer. Ballentree laid his ear against his chest; a heartbeat was there.

The deputy hefted Crosston onto his shoulders. Grunting under the weight, he moved toward the door. His foot slid in blood; he staggered and had to step back to balance himself. In the process Ballentree kicked over the cup. Blood drained across the floor in a livid scarlet flood.

The deputy suffered an assault of squeamishness

and had to close his eyes for a moment. Then he carried Crosston's limp body out the door and down the hallway, balancing Crosston as he made his way into the street. He brought the Englishman to the office of an aging doctor named Seward, whom he roused with kicks against the door.

A half hour later Dr. Seward, white hair askew and backlit by a coal-oil lamp perched nearby, was half finished with the stitching of John Crosston's arm. Ballentree watched from the corner.

"This one meant business," Seward said. "Good thing you found him when you did. Otherwise he would be dead by now."

"Will he make it, Doc?"

"Can't say."

"Strange to run into him again." Ballentree spoke like a man thinking aloud.

"You know him?" asked the doctor.

Ballentree flushed; suddenly he was embarrassed. "In a way. I met him once, before I came to Helena."

"I see. You were where? Oh yes. Henley, up in the Bitterroots."

"Yes."

"I hear you had some interesting times there. Even met Simon Caine."

Ballentree mumbled: "Yes, I met him."

"Now there's a murdering heathen if ever there was one. You're lucky he didn't scalp you, Deputy. I hear tell he's done that a time or two."

"He has."

"Tell me, what's he like?"

Ballentree had to stifle a burst of anger at the doctor's gossip mongering.

"I don't know what he's like," he said. "I spent a few hours with him in my jail, that's all. Now if you'll pardon me, Doc, I need to get back over to the hotel and look over that room. If your patient there wakes up, let me know. By the way, he's wanted, so watch him."

The doctor turned. "Wanted? For what?"

"Murder."

Ballentree left the office and returned to the Montana House. The place was astir, its residents awake and talking about what had happened. Ballentree mounted the steps and entered the room where Crosston had been, angrily ordering out two gapers who had come inside it.

Landers appeared at the door. "May I come in?"

"Come on," Ballentree said. He was looking at the blood on the floor, the shattered bottle, and the overturned chalice.

"I can't believe this," Landers said. "Nothing like it ever has happened in my hotel. My business doesn't need this sort of thing."

Ballentree stooped and picked up the bottle fragment by the bed. "Ripped his own arm open with this, Ben. Not just a little cut, either. All the way up his forearm."

"Why did he do it?"

"That I don't know. He sure wanted to die."

Ballentree picked up the bloody cup. He raised it and eyed it curiously.

"What's that?" Landers asked.

Ballentree shook his head. "Evidence. That's what you call it when you can't say what it is."

The deputy swabbed out the blood with a corner of the sheet. "Don't give me that look, Ben. Sheet's bloody, anyway. Close up this room and don't let anybody in. And don't you think about cleaning it yet. We'll be back."

Ballentree wandered alone onto the street. He moved slowly back toward the doctor's office, not wanting to hurry. He needed to think.

He paused on a porch and leaned against a rail. He sat the cup at his feet, then cut a cud of tobacco and settled it into his jaw. Sucking at it, he let the strong taste burn tongue and throat.

Simon Caine—if he was nearby earlier tonight, where was he now? In some shadowed corner a throw's distance away? Ballentree frowned. God, he didn't want to see that face again.

It wasn't out of fear, strangely, though Ballentree knew Caine would kill him without hesitation if given cause. But that was the point. Caine hadn't killed Ballentree, even though he had had two good chances.

It was a funny thing. All the stories said Caine was a man without a heart, utterly compassionless. But in Ballentree's case it had not proven so. And that had nagged at the lawman ever since.

The dime novels and the saloon storytellers portrayed Caine either as a heroic figure—if the storyteller was an unreconstructed southerner—or as a murderer devoid of any worth or kindness.

I'll bet you're not either one, Ballentree thought. I'll bet you're just a man who stumbled into hell and lost his way trying to get out again.

Ballentree spit tobacco and shifted his foot. Accidentally, he kicked over the chalice, and it rolled off the porch into the street.

23

William Montrose heard the slow plodding of a weary horse that drew near outside his house. He picked up a derringer, palmed it, went to the door, slid back the cover of a small view hole and looked out. Montrose dropped the derringer into his pocket and threw open the door.

Brannigan looked like a nearly dead man on a nearly dead horse. His face was almost gray and his eyes were wild with pain. Leaning forward, he gripped his right arm tightly across his chest. It was obvious that every breath brought suffering. Bloodstains crusted his shirt and his beard.

"Montrose, help me," he said. He fell from the saddle and hit the ground with a hard thud.

Montrose looked down at him, his lip curled. He shook his head, laid his finger across his nostrils to block the stench of the fallen bounty hunter and shouted for aid. Two of his men came at a run.

Brannigan would have slept a long time on the feather tick upon which they placed him, but Montrose would not allow it. The bounty hunter wakened with a cry of pain as Montrose shook him.

"Where is Simon Caine?"

"Where he always will be."

"Talk straight to me or I'll kill you right here."

"You'll never catch Caine," Brannigan said. "Nobody will ever catch him."

Montrose pulled away for a second, then his eyes sparked and his lips went tight. He drew back his fist, but did not follow through. Instead, he wheeled and walked away. Pausing by a bookshelf, he reached up and took the scalp lock of his brother. He fingered the stiff hair, the parchmentlike flesh. When his temper had cooled, he turned.

"What happened to you?" he asked quietly.

"I don't know," Brannigan said. "Something got me. Something from a cave."

"What? A wolf, a bear—"

Brannigan shook his head. "Something else." He paused, then said: "The redskins say there's a spirit or a devil or such up there."

Montrose looked at him intently, then laughed. "A spirit? I sent you to get Simon Caine and you come back telling me ghost stories?"

"I saw it. More than saw it—look what it did to me! Cracked my ribs, threw me over a bluff. I crawled away, finally found a horse, made it back here."

"And what of Caine?"

"I had him, but the . . . thing—it protected him. The man can't be taken, Montrose. Leave him be."

"What about the others?" Montrose said. "Where are they—and the money?"

"Dead. All of them dead. The money's lost."

Montrose glowered, and nodded at two men who stood near the door. They went to Brannigan. One struck the bounty hunter across the mouth. The other pounded his elbow into his cracked ribs. Brannigan screamed and passed out.

One of the men dug into Brannigan's pockets but found nothing.

"Get rid of him," Montrose said in disgust.

They hefted up the broken, senseless man and carried him back to his horse. They threw him over the back of the unsaddled animal, brought out a rope and lashed him down.

One man drew his pistol and pointed it to the sky. "Wait," the other said. "It seems right cruel to send him off like that in the shape he is. Wait a minute."

The man reentered the house, and half a minute later came back out with a paper in his hand. He attached it to the back of Brannigan's shirt. The other read it aloud: "This man needs a doctor." He laughed and fired the pistol. The horse ran down the hill, through the town, and vanished into the forest.

Caine heard the voice of a child slice through the murk of his sleep. He moved, feeling the roughness of the straw tick against his back. His eyes opened just enough to see morning sunlight shafting in at a familiar angle. He heard the child's voice again. Marcus, up early for a Saturday morning. Simon Caine reached across to Nancy.

He opened his eyes and, for what seemed the millionth time, suffered the stab of reality. He was not on his bed back in Tennessee, but on his blanket spread atop loose hay in a barn loft. The sunlight that poured in came not through his bedroom window, but through a ventilation hole in the barn wall. He closed his eyes and wished he could sleep again. In sleep it was, sometimes, as if he were with them. Awake, he always was alone.

"Mister, I said wake up."

The child's voice again. Caine sat up. A red-haired

boy with his hands wrapped tightly around an old percussion-cap rifle looked up at him, his freckles spangled across a scared white face.

"You just sit still. My pa, he'll be here in a minute with the others."

"Son, I've intruded in your barn, but I meant no harm. You just lay down that rifle and I'll be gone."

"No sir. My brother's run to get Pa and the others, and they'll be here directly."

Pa and the others was a group Caine was not eager to meet, but he couldn't ignore the boy's rifle.

"How old are you, son?"

"I'm near twelve. Man enough to shoot this thing, if that's what you're getting at."

"I'd say you are. You know, son, I had a boy once. He was a handsome young fellow, just like you."

In truth, the redheaded little rifleman was quite homely, but Caine's compliment seemed well taken. The boy eased his grip on the rifle just a trace.

"What's your boy's name?" he asked.

"Marcus," Caine said. "We called him Mark. Like the man in the Bible."

"Yeah. Is he somewhere around here?"

"No. My boy's dead. Died years ago, even before he was old as you."

The boy didn't seem to know what to say to that. Finally he asked: "He get sick?"

"No. He got . . . hurt. Hurt bad enough to die."

"I'm sorry, then. But I'll still shoot you if you move."

"Reckon you would."

Outside Caine heard horsemen. He looked through a knothole. There was a small army approaching out there. Cattlemen, from the look of them, armed and looking frightfully serious.

The boy grinned. "I told you they'd be here."

The riders moved around the barn and five or six dismounted. They came into the barn, guns ready, and surrounded the boy.

"You did a brave thing, Clarence. I'm proud of you," said a man whose hair rivaled the boy's in brilliance. He gazed up with pinhole eyes, twin islands in a sea of freckles.

"Mister, you just sit still," he commanded. "Shadrach, is this the one you seen?"

Another appeared, a bald man with a head round as a billiard ball. He squinted at Caine.

"No," he finally said. "No way this is the one. I told you, Will, he wasn't no regular-looking human being. He was half bear."

The redheaded man lowered his gun and his brows at the same time. "Who you be?" he demanded of Caine.

"A traveler. I needed a place to sleep, and I figured I'd be out of everybody's way in this loft."

The man shrugged and chewed his lip. "It's my barn and my loft, and I don't run it for no hotel, but there's no harm done. Sorry about the ruckus, friend. There's been trouble last night, and me and Shadrach and these here others have been out looking since sunup. When my boy here"—he indicated a slightly older version of the first lad—"come saying there was somebody in the barn, we just kind of got nervous. You're lucky it was us that found you and not the one we're after, though."

"Why?"

"We're not sure it's really a man. I know that sounds crazy, but Shadrach seen him and swears that . . . well, you just heard him yourself. He saw this . . . thing in his chicken pen, just ripping open a live hen

146

like it was a bread load. Ate at it all raw and bloody. Something bad wrong with a man who would do that, if it is a man."

Caine recognized the singular description, but Gideon? The giant he'd seen; the one mentioned in Crosston's journal? He didn't let the others see his reaction.

"I'll be getting out of your barn now. I'm obliged for the use of it."

"What's your name?" came a voice from below. Caine's heart raced. Mentally, he began mapping out a plan—who would take the first shot, who the second, which way would be the best to leap from the loft . . .

"Robert Cole," he said.

"Would you mind moving into the light where I can see you?" Caine moved to the edge of the loft and looked down.

"I've seen you before, Mr. Cole. Can't recall where. Ernest, you recognize him?"

Another man scrutinized him, then shook his head. "Don't reckon I have," he said.

The other man frowned, still suspicious. "Just can't put my finger on it," he said.

"Why don't you just go on, Mr. Cole," said the red-haired leader. "But if you're traveling alone, I suggest you be careful. The one we're looking for is big and likely to be mean. If you want to join us, you may. We're going into Helena to get the law."

"Thanks, but I'll just ride on."

Caine recovered his mount from the meadow where he had hobbled it and rode away, feeling their eyes on him.

"One man, but that's all," said the marshal to the cluster of men in his office. "One's all I can spare.

147

Why are you so worked up, anyway? Crazy man tears apart a chicken and you expect me to deputize the whole population?"

"First a chicken, then maybe a child, Joe," said the red-haired man. "We told you, this was no ordinary man. He was big as a mountain. His track was wide as my head, and that's no lie. Maybe it's not a man at all, but some kind of animal that nobody's seen yet."

"Aw, get off that foolishness," the marshal said. "You get your bowels in an uproar over every little thing. One man's all you're getting. That'll be you, Ballentree."

Jim Ballentree looked reluctant. "Marshal, with the prisoner over at Doc Seward's, I think—"

"We can watch him just as good as you, Deputy. You're the new man, so you chase the chicken kill-ers. We'll make sure your Englisher stays put."

"Yes, sir." Ballentree turned to another deputy, who was smiling his seniority. "Wilbur, if you would—"

"I'll tell your wife you won't be on time again," the other said.

When they were out of town, Ballentree had the riders take him to where the big man had been seen. When he saw the footprints in the mud, the mission suddenly didn't seem so trivial.

The print was huge—not as big as the man had implied back at the office, but definitely bigger than any Ballentree had seen before.

"One thing we can know: it is a man," he said. "That's a moccasin track."

One of the others asked: "What kind of man would do this?" He gestured at a scattering of bloodied feathers on the ground.

"A very hungry one, I suppose," Ballentree said.

"Well, we'd best find him. There's good tracks here. Why didn't you follow these on your own?"

The leader looked sheepish. "Got a little skittish, I admit. Started out after him, then decided we'd best get the law. We never found anything but a stranger in my barn."

"A stranger?"

"Tall fellow. Looked like a mountaineer. He said his name was Cole."

Ballentree was thoughtful a moment. "Let's get started," he said.

They rode through the late-morning light, following a trail that seemed to lead nowhere and often circled back upon itself. It was the track of a man lost, wandering.

They paused for a bite at noon, then continued. The trail led into high, rocky country. Then it disappeared along a dry streambed. Ballentree dismounted and searched the ground. Nothing.

"He's gotten away," he said. "We'll never find him in these high rocks."

He stood, slapping dust from his hands, staring up at the ridgeline. "We could try circling and—" His voice caught in his throat.

High above, silhouetted against the sky, was a rider. A distinctive, lean form of a man. Though the distance was too great to let him discern the rider's features, Jim Ballentree knew who it was.

The rider on the ridge turned his mount and was gone.

"What is it, Deputy?" one of the others asked.

"Nothing," Ballentree said. "We'd best turn back."

24

Gideon hardly walked now. He merely groped his way through the rocks, moving on only because he could find no place nor reason to stop. The pain he had endured so long was almost unbearable. He finally fell, dropping to his hands and knees, then onto his face. He rolled onto his back, grimacing at the sun.

He was unconscious when Simon Caine's shadow blocked the light from his face. The outlaw knelt over the fallen man.

"Did you think I could bring it back to you? Is that why you followed me?" Caine felt for and found Gideon's pulse, then nodded. "It's going to be all right now," he said.

Back from his fruitless search, Ballentree sat alone in the doctor's office, staring into the corner. His duty was to guard John Crosston, but his mind was not on it. He remembered the image of Simon Caine against the sky, and mulled over this unexpected repetition of the past.

The chalice stood at his feet. He had been toying with it since this morning. After yesterday's sighting, thoughts of Caine had stolen his night's rest. Weary today, he sat heavily in his straight-back chair by the doctor's bottle-laden cabinet, turning the cup in his hands, sometimes dozing.

The old chalice was a fascinating piece of refuse. Ballentree had picked it up at the marshal's office this morning, planning to ask Crosston to identify it, but so far he hadn't, for Crosston had been asleep.

Ballentree's head bobbed and his eyes drooped and shut. He began to snore.

"Deputy?"

The voice was soft, almost tremulous. Ballentree awakened with a start and stared into the eyes of John Crosston.

"May I have it?" the Englishman asked, extending his hands. His face was of an almost ghoulish palor, his hair matted and eyes red. He shook where he stood.

"What are you doing up? The doctor said you couldn't even stand."

"I hardly can," whispered the other. "But I need the cup."

Ballentree handed it to Crosston, who smiled feebly. He cradled the chalice gently.

Crosston glanced up at Ballentree. "I know you," he said. "From the jail in Henley."

"Yes."

"I'm sorry about striking you. I had no choice."

"Who are you, Crosston? And what is this thing?"

The Englishman staggered. Weakly, he made for another chair. He fell into it, breathing heavily, still holding the cup.

"What is it?" repeated Ballentree.

"Nothing."

Ballentree stood. "You need to be back in bed. Let me help you."

Crosston stood with Ballentree's help. "I'm dizzy," he said. Ballentree helped Crosston into the bed. The young man sank his head into the sweaty pillow and gasped deeply. He held the chalice across his chest. Ballentree could see the scabbed gash down his arm. Crosston looked like a corpse, but for his shuddering breathing.

Ballentree turned away, wanting to be away from the stench and pallor of this man. He returned to his chair, but grew restless. He stood and walked to the windowed door. He pulled aside the yellow curtain and looked out.

He was alone in the office. The doctor had been called out in mid-afternoon; now it was beginning to darken and he was not yet back. Ballentree wished he would return. Being in the office with a delirious, breathing-and-pulsing cadaver was unnerving.

Ballentree turned, digging into his pocket for a match to light a lamp. Crosston stood no more than a yard away, with the doctor's heavy mortar raised in his hands. He brought it down hard, and Ballentree fell senseless.

A pale dawn light touched Helena's streets as Simon Caine walked slowly into town, leading his travois-burdened horse. In this early hour only a few saw the strange pair from the wilderness—the blacksmith early at the forge, a laundryman, Old Bailey the drunk, lounging in an alley.

From the opposite end of town a buggy rolled in, carrying the exhausted Dr. Seward, returning from a delivery of twins. He saw Caine and his cargo approaching as he drew near his office. He halted his buggy and waited until they reached him.

"Are you the doctor here?" Caine asked.

"I am. What's wrong with that . . . man?" The doctor had noticed the size of Gideon.

"He's shot. You got to help him."

"Who is he?"

"His name is Gideon."

Caine unhitched the travois, and together he and the doctor struggled with the huge body. The doctor pounded on the door and called for Ballentree.

The door creaked open and Ballentree's face appeared. It was bloody. The deputy clung to the doorframe to keep on his feet.

Doc Seward could only shake his head. He recalled what he had been told in student days: a doctor's business was like summer rain—little for a long time, then a flood.

"He's gone," Ballentree said. "Hit me—now he's gone."

Then Ballentree saw Simon Caine. The lawman and the outlaw stared at each other.

"I'll tend to you later," the doctor said. "We've got one a lot worse right here."

Caine and the doctor carried Gideon inside and laid him on the bed where Crosston had been. The bedframe creaked under the weight. Caine laid his hand on Gideon's shoulder.

Ballentree went to his chair and sat down, cupping his head in his hands, not sure whether he was about to be sick or burst into laughter.

25

The doctor, shadowed by Caine, worked on Gideon's festering wound. Gideon's broad face was calm and he breathed steadily despite the doctor's probings.

"Who is this man?" Doc Seward asked. "Where did he come from?"

"From the mountains," Caine replied. "He's just . . . what he is."

"And what's that?"

Caine did not know how to answer. He watched the doctor awhile longer, then walked into the front room.

Ballentree followed him. "I'm going after Crosston," he said.

"You're in no shape for it," Caine returned.

"I'll make it. He's in no shape to get far, either." But as Ballentree stepped toward the door, he stumbled to one side.

"I'll go after him," Caine said.

"No. I'm the law here. He's my prisoner."

"I've got more cause than you to go after him," Caine said.

"You're a wanted man, Caine. I don't know your connection with Crosston, but you might be in league with him. Or maybe you'll kill him."

"I'm not in league with him, and if I wanted to kill him, I would have already."

Ballentree straightened again, but was unsteady on his feet. "I've got to stop you, Caine."

"I don't believe you will."

Ballentree drew and leveled his pistol. "I don't want to do this. But I've got duties."

Caine was calm. "I'm going after John Crosston. And you're not going to stop me, Deputy. We're not going to hurt each other."

Ballentree, after hesitation, lowered his pistol. "No, we're not."

"Was he armed?" Caine asked.

"No. He didn't even take my pistol, as you can see." Ballentree leaned against the wall and touched his scalp gingerly. "All he took was that cup of his."

"He's got the cup?"

"Yes. What is that thing, anyway?"

"Something Crosston has no right to. It's Gideon's."

Ballentree wanted to know more, but Caine walked past him and out the door, so there was no time to ask. Ballentree stood alone, marveling at the fact he again had let Caine get away from him.

There was blood on the porch. Caine had learned from the doctor what Crosston had done to himself. The blood indicated Crosston had reopened the wound in his arm and was again losing blood. He could not go far.

Caine mounted and rode slowly down the street, picking out Crosston's footprints and the rusty bloodstains coagulating in the dirt around them.

Outside of town he dismounted and studied the ground. Finding Crosston's sign amid the pounded hoofprints and bootmarks, he once more mounted and followed.

The trail became a path cutting down into a narrow valley heavy with trees and undergrowth, until finally, a hundred yards away, he saw an old log house, apparently long abandoned. Outside it was a small cemetery plot with six tombstones standing crooked among weeds. Crosston was there, leaning against one of them, watching himself bleed to death as he clutched the cup.

Caine walked through the rotting cemetery gate and stopped.

"I tore it open when I got up," Crosston said, looking at his arm. "They had sewed it up, but I tore it open again." He spoke without obvious emotion. "Bleeding like ruddy hell," he said.

He pulled the chalice close. "I've got to keep the cup. I thought about it as I lay there—I know it isn't real, but maybe I can convince my father it is. I don't care if it's a lie. I want him to be happy."

Caine said, "Did you really think you could survive in the shape you're in?"

Crosston smiled sadly and shook his head. "I had to try."

Caine said, "I can't let you keep the cup. There's one who's got more of a right to it than you ever will."

"No," Crosston said. "It's mine." But his eyes glazed for a moment and the chalice slid to the ground. "Too weak to hold it," he said, his voice scarcely audible.

"Let me take you back," Caine said. "The doctor can stop the bleeding, maybe save your life."

"Why should you care, Caine?"

"A man can't kill forever."

"It's too late for me," Crosston said. "They'd just take the cup from me."

"It's your choice," Caine said. "But I'm taking the cup."

Crosston closed his eyes and leaned to one side. His wounded arm fell limply across his thigh, blood coming out now in slow, erratic spurts.

"Crosston?"

No response. The Englishman's body slid to the earth. He stopped breathing. Caine went to him and opened one of his eyes. The orb had the luster of cold marble and the pupil was fixed. No more blood came from his arm.

Caine picked up the cup and returned to town.

When he arrived back at the doctor's office, he found Gideon resting on the sickbed in the back room. Beside him stood Jim Ballentree and the town marshal. A third man stood back in the corner. Caine recognized him as one of the band that had questioned him at gunpoint in the barn loft.

The man looked fearfully at Caine. His dry tongue licked over his lips and his hands trembled on the brim of the hat he clutched.

"Howdy, mister," the marshal said to Caine. "I need to talk to you."

"Then talk."

"What's your name?"

"Robert Cole."

"You sure of that?"

"A man's generally sure of his own name." Caine glanced at Ballentree; the deputy looked like he was about to pass out.

"Mr. Cole, I got a man here who says you're Simon Caine. Says he seen you in the Battle of Saltville."

"Well, if I was Simon Caine, I reckon you would be living out your last moments right about now."

The words bore a cold sting the marshal took without reaction, other than a subtle narrowing of his eyes. "We can get this straightened out easy enough," he said. "Jim, is that the man you had in your jail in Henley?"

Ballentree looked into Caine's face. In his mind duties battled duties, instincts and thoughts tangled into knots. When he spoke, it was like hearing someone else say the words: "I'd know Simon Caine if I saw him again, Marshal."

The marshal thought for a moment. "You would at that, Jim."

26

"So his father killed himself, eh?" Montrose said.

"That he did," said Morrison DeGuere. "When the police found him, he had a newspaper clipping in his hand—a story about the arrest of the swindler who had sold him the cup years before. It seems the man had been at it for years—cheating the rich with various swindles, most of them involving the sale of antiquities of supposed great rarity and value. When old Crosston found out he had been fooled, he apparently couldn't handle it. Wrote a letter, had his servant mail it, then put a hole through his head."

"A letter?"

"To his son, I suspect. My associate talked to the servant who mailed it. The servant can't read, so he didn't know who it was addressed to, or where."

Montrose shook his head. He took the scalp lock from his pocket. DeGuere watched him touch it, feel it—it was becoming a habit with Montrose, though Montrose obviously didn't even realize it.

"The man was a fool—his son too," Montrose said. "The very idea of such a relic surviving all those years, being carried all this distance—it's preposterous."

DeGuere said, "So it would appear. But there's the

159

strangest twist in this whole affair. The swindler has confessed to more than two dozen outright frauds, but he swears the Grail is real. Nobody believes him, of course."

"Of course."

DeGuere leaned back in his chair and linked his fingers behind his head. "What's next, William? Will you hire another bounty hunter to try to bring back Caine?"

"No," Montrose said. "Not a bounty hunter. A detective."

DeGuere smiled. "A good decision. But a detective on such a job would require high pay—"

"He will be paid well," Montrose said. "But only if he succeeds. I want Simon Caine dead, Morrison. Whatever you have to do, wherever you have to go—I want Simon Caine."

DeGuere said, "It might take time. The word is that Caine has left the mountains."

"You can find him."

"Yes."

Montrose poured whiskey for both of them. He raised his glass. "To the death of Simon Caine."

"Hear, hear."

And they drank.

Caine placed the chalice into the hands of Gideon as he slept. The big man clutched it tight, as if by instinct. His breathing deepened and he seemed to relax.

"Where is Crosston?" Ballentree asked.

"He died east of town in an old graveyard. I left him there."

Ballentree looked down at the chalice. It moved with Gideon's breathing. "What is it, Caine?"

"Just an old cup."

"But who is this man? And what's his interest in it?"

"His name is Gideon. He guards the cup. Protects it. It's his way of serving God, I think. Some of us serve. Some of us run."

Ballentree lowered his head. "What I did wasn't right. I'm a deputy, and I've got duties."

"We've all got duties. Some real, some we just dream up and spend our lives chasing after. Or letting them chase after us. I'm not sure I know much about it anymore. The older I get, the less I seem to know about most things."

"What will you do now?"

"Just keep moving."

"Talk in Henley was you'd go back and kill Will Montrose someday."

"No," said Caine. "Just don't seem worth it anymore."

"You'll go back to the Bitterroots?"

"No. Maybe I'll go find my brother, if I can."

"I hope you do," Ballentree said. "A man can't run forever."

"No. But he can try."

Caine rode out of Helena the way he had come. Only as he left Ballentree's sight did the deputy realize he never had explained the cup.

Three days passed, then four, and Gideon still hung onto his chalice and his life. The doctor was astounded. The big man should have been dead.

On the fifth day Gideon was much stronger, so much so that the doctor could no longer wrestle the cup from his grasp. At last the doctor began to see there was a connection between it and Gideon's tenacity of life, and after that he left it alone.

On the seventh day Gideon was gone. He had squeezed out a window in the night and had taken his cup with him.

Jim Ballentree traced Gideon's sign a couple of miles. He had headed west toward the Bitterroots.

HISTORICAL END NOTE

The character of Simon Caine is fictitious, but his inspiration comes from a historical figure out of Middle Tennessee's Civil War years—a Confederate bushwhacker named Champ Ferguson. Ferguson was a violent, bloodletting man who, according to some reports, killed more than a hundred men during the war. Legend has it he began his wholesale killing career, like Simon Caine, in revenge for a Union atrocity.

Depending upon the source, one can find two versions of the purported offense that made Ferguson become a bushwhacker. One story claims that after the war began, eleven Unionist neighbors of Ferguson entered his home while he was away, forced his wife and daughter to disrobe and cook a meal for them in the nude, then drove the humiliated pair, still unclothed, down a public road. A more melodramatic story claims Ferguson's small son was murdered by passing Union soldiers after the boy waved a small Confederate flag at them from the front porch of the family home.

Colorful as those legends are, neither is likely to be true. A more probable explanation for Ferguson's activity is the one he gave himself: He was promised by Confederate sympathizers that murder charges against him in a neighboring county would be dropped if he would side with the South.

Ferguson's base of operations was the Calfkiller River valley of Middle Tennessee. From there he led irregular fighters into East Tennessee, Kentucky, and Virginia, battling both regular federal troops and Union guerilla bands. A particular foe was "Tinker Dave" Beatty, a farmer from nearby Fentress County, who decided to fight against rather than run from Ferguson and his like. A body of folklore exists describing various encounters between Ferguson and Tinker Dave.

Ferguson and his cohorts were heartless killers. In 1864, for example, he shot to death a federal prisoner who lay wounded in a military hospital bed. In the Battle of Dug Hill, fought near Ferguson's home with him as participant, Confederate bushwhackers with Ferguson killed three captured Union troops by smashing their skulls with rocks. It was a cruel execution, but the bushwhackers were trying to save ammunition.

Unlike his fictional semicounterpart Caine, Ferguson did not evade legal reprisal for his actions. In May 1865 federal troops arrested him at his home in White County and took him to a military prison in Nashville. He was tried before a military commission; the hearing lasted from mid-July to mid-September. He was charged with being a guerilla and with murdering fifty-three people, including the aforementioned military prisoner. No one was surprised when he was found guilty.

On October 20 guards escorted Ferguson to a scaffold in the Nashville military prison, and there more than twenty of the charges against him were read (one eyewitness reported that Ferguson nodded as some of his crimes were recounted, and at one point said, "I could tell it better than that"). Ferguson's final request was to be buried near his home on the Calfkiller.

As his wife and daughter watched, Ferguson was hanged. His family took his corpse to the Old France cemetery in the valley of the Calfkiller and there buried it. His grave remains clearly marked today.

Cameron Judd
September 26, 1987

ABOUT THE AUTHOR

I was born in 1956 in Tennessee, the state in which I have lived all my life. I wrote my first western at age twenty-two and now I am writing exclusively for Bantam.

My interest in the American West is part of a broader interest in the frontier. I am fascinated by the vast westward expanses on the other side of the Mississippi, but I am equally intrigued by the original American West: the area west of the Appalachians and east of the Mississippi. I hope someday to write fiction set in that older frontier at the time of its settlement, in addition to traditional westerns.

My interest in westerns was sparked in early childhood by television, movies, and books. I love both the fact of the West and the myth of the West; both aspects have a valid place in popular fiction.

I received an undergraduate degree in English and journalism, plus teaching accreditation in English and history, from Tennessee Technological University in 1979. Since that time I have been a newspaper journalist by profession, both as a writer and editor. Today I live near Greeneville, Tennessee, one of the state's most historic towns. Greeneville is the seat of the county that contributed one of America's original frontier heroes to the world—Davy Crockett. Greeneville was also the hometown of President Andrew Johnson and was for several years the capital of the Lost State of Franklin—an eighteenth-century political experiment that came close to achieving statehood.

My home is in rural Greene County. My wife, Rhonda, and I have three children, Matthew, Laura, and Bonnie.

If you enjoyed Cameron Judd's action-packed saga of the untamed American West, be sure to look for his next book, **JERUSALEM CAMP**, at your local bookstore. Cameron Judd is one of the most promising young writers in the field of Western adventure.

Here's an exciting preview of the next book
from Cameron Judd

JERUSALEM CAMP

On sale in July, wherever Bantam Books are sold

Chapter 1

He came to the mountains as the snow fell, and the clip of his big bay's hooves marked off the changing of the seasons. Later, the people of Jerusalem Camp would recall his time among them as the Killing Winter. The man himself they would recall only by the single name he gave them, for he never gave another, and when at last he rode out again with a new season at his heels, he rode out for good.

He climbed the Sierras with a bullet crease in his leg and the two armed riders who had put it there close behind him. He pushed the bay along canyon flanks, beneath granite cliffs, and up washes lined with tamarack and sugar pine. Gray clouds spat snow that piled thickly on the ground and hampered the bay. The rider looked back frequently, and bent low, perhaps from pain, perhaps just to make himself less conspicuous.

He slowed when he reached a snow-encrusted stand of pine that was so closely bunched his horse could barely push through. When at last it did and then ascended a slope, the rider looked back and saw his pursuers already coming through the stand. Too close. He spurred his horse, but the weary animal, sides heaving and nostrils spewing steam, could go no faster.

On a jumble of talus at the base of a black escarpment, the bay stepped into a hole and pitched, whinnying, to the left. As the rider fell painfully on rock shards, he heard the snap of the horse's left foreleg.

He rose and wiped blood from his shattered lip into his sleeve. He glanced once into the tormented eyes of his fallen horse and vainly wished he had the time and spare ammunition to end the beast's suffering.

In the cold air a shot from behind him made a flat, slapping sound that echoed off the escarpment. He struggled forward, came to a ravine, and leapt into it. He pulled icy air into his lungs; it burned like cold fire.

He looked at his wounded leg: still bleeding. At least it didn't hurt. The strain and the cold had numbed him so he did not feel it, the snow beneath his thin boot soles, or the slice of the wind through his canvas trousers.

He scrambled along the ravine, but his progress was too slow. So, gritting his teeth, he rolled up out of it on his back and belly. He stood and was surprised to see four men before him. Strangers, armed. They had just emerged from a scraggly forest of pine a hundred feet ahead.

Another shot sounded behind him; the bullet zipped over his head. One of the strangers ahead raised a rifle and fired back. The lone man was caught in the middle.

He dropped back into the ravine, his face digging into the snow. He heard more gunfire back and forth, then suddenly it stopped. For several seconds, the Sierras were utterly silent. The man cautiously stood and peered over the edge of the ravine. The four from the forest approached, rifles smoking. He glanced behind; his pursuers were gone.

He smiled as the four men reached him, and said, "I'm obliged—" but one of the men drew back his rifle, brought down the butt, and knocked him cold.

The four men gathered around the edge of the ravine and looked at his still form, silent as their breath made white fog in the mountain and fear they dared not reveal tasted like bile in their throats.

Jared learned of the capture from Jimmy Essler, a boy who lived several houses up from his forge. The gap-toothed boy was very excited and lisped it out to the blacksmith like this: "Mither Cable, they got a man caught and down at Mither Rupert and Mither Rupert ith ready to hang him!"

"What? Hang who?"

"The man! They caught the man!"

Jared saw that he would gain no understanding from Jimmy, so he hurriedly dusted off his hands, doffed his leather smith's apron, and slipped on his coat. The smithy was hot, but outside the snow churned down in a near-blizzard and the twilight air was biting cold.

Jimmy came out at Jared's heels and passed him at a dead run through the contorted field of white. The flakes fell so thickly that before Jimmy was twenty feet ahead Jared lost sight of him.

Rupert's was a store in one way of looking at it, and a saloon and gambling house in another. Loren Rupert was dedicated to keeping vice alive in Jerusalem Camp, a purpose that had set him firmly against Jared Cable's preacher father ever since Rupert had drifted up from the American River camps years ago. Now that Jared had accepted the mostly symbolic job of town marshal, he suspected that he was replacing his aging father as Rupert's chief object of wrath.

Rupert's door tended to jam, then pop open loudly, so when Jared entered he got the full attention of every man inside. It was a solemn gathering: Rupert and four no-goods who hung around his place. Jimmy Essler was there, too, having scrambled in ahead of Jared. Jared smelled the familiar mix of hot coffee, woodsmoke, chalk dust, and whiskey that permeated the building.

Rupert, his gray and black hair slick with bay rum, said with thick, smiling sarcasm. "Well, look here, boys. It's the marshal."

"Hello, Loren," Jared said. He looked down at Jimmy, whose red hair was growing damp as the snow flecked on it melted in the heat of Rupert's pine-fed stove. "Boy, you'd best get on before your ma worries."

"Aw, c'mon, Mither Cable," the boy complained. "Anytime anything geth tharted I get thent off."

"Get on," Jared repeated.

The boy's face darkened, but immediately brightened. "I know what I'll do," he said. He opened the door and vanished as before into the white swirl.

Jared said, "The boy mentioned something about a man, and a hanging—"

Clyde Ingersoll, whose bulbous nose might have been red from cold but more likely from something else, said, "This ain't your business, Cable."

"You got a man here or not?" Jared demanded. Rupert gave an almost mischievous grin. "We do."

"Where?"

Rupert thumbed toward a storage room behind him.

Jared entered. The rider lay on the bare floor. He

had been unconscious, but was starting to rouse.

"Who is he?" Jared asked.

"How should I know?" Rupert said. "We caught him coming in toward town with two men shooting at him. We took it they might be shooting at us, too, and shot back. He's the one we're after—that I'll wager."

"Now how do you know that?"

"Who else could he be?"

Jared shook his head. "You never fail to astound me, Rupert. Not a shred of evidence and you're ready to string up a man just because he rode through at the wrong time." Jared paused when he saw the blood on the man's trousers. "You've shot him!"

"He was shot before we ever seen him," Rupert said defensively. "It's just a crease. And nobody's said nothing about stringing him up. That was just the boy talking."

"I'll bet."

Jared briefly searched the man's pockets, looking for identification. He found nothing, but he noted a leather string around the man's neck, extending below his shirt. Jared pulled it out. On it hung an oval brass medallion, worn nearly smooth so its image of a tree and a river was now only scarcely visible.

"What's that?" Rupert asked, Jared shook his head.

Behind them the balky door popped open again and Logan Hull entered. Doc Hull, the townsfolk called him, though his medical credentials didn't strictly justify it. He had worked in field hospitals during the war with Mexico—an effective school of medicine, but one that issued no diplomas or shingles to swing above doors.

Doc Hull walked into the back room and knelt

beside the supine man, whose eyes fluttered open a second later. The others regrouped around him. The man looked around the room, resting his gaze for a moment on each face. Doc said, "Easy, my friend. I'm a doctor. Let me check you."

"How'd you hear about this, Doc?" Jared asked.

"Jimmy Essler just now told me. I sent him home."

Hull prodded the furrowed bullet wound. The man winced.

"Sorry, son," Doc said. "I'm just checking on—"

With speed that surprised them all, the man burst upward. He pushed back Hull, who fell on his rump. A fast swing brought down Ingersoll, and the follow-through hammered Rupert's jaw with a sound like a cracking walnut. The store owner staggered, flailed out for a handhold, and grabbed the hot pipe of his wood-stove. He screeched, let go, and fell atop Ingersoll.

Rupert's other cronies yelled and leapt away. Wild-eyed, the stranger brought back his fist and charged at Jared.

The man was fast, but Jared, spurred by surprise, was faster. He rolled up a fist big as a muskmelon and drove it bullet-straight into the stranger's mouth. The man's legs went soft, and he fell to his knees, teetered for a second with his arms limp at his sides, then pitched facedown onto the floor, once again out cold.

Two men stood shivering on the snow-whipped mountain wilderness. One said, "We're lost. Sooner we admit it and get to town, the better."

"A group from that town shot at us, Joe. It wouldn't be sensible."

"Is it sensible to freeze to death?"

The other had no answer. All about them snow blotted the horizon, making every direction the same. Finally, the one named Joe said what both had been unwillingly thinking. "We'll be like the Donner party if we don't get to shelter. Maybe we should go back to the cabin with Frank."

Mansell looked around at the deathly white. His horse stamped and pawed in the snow. "Forget about Frank," he said. "We'd never find the way there anyway. We'll try for the town. It lies yonder."

The other frowned. "I thought it was that way—"

"Yonder," Mansell said emphatically. But he wasn't as sure as he sounded.

They plunged forward, leading their mounts, stepping high in the rising drifts. The effort was three times harder than it would have been on bare ground, and their hearts hammered at their ribs. Joe screwed his hat low in a vain effort to shield ears so cold he couldn't even tell without feeling for them that they were still there. As they moved, terribly slowly, the day waned. Night slid over the sky like thick gray paint.

"We're going to die out here," Joe said.

"Shut up."

After fifteen minutes, neither could tell how far they had gone, nor if they had traveled straight or merely circled. Nor in which direction lay Jerusalem Camp. They plodded on as the snow piled to their knees.

At last they reached a clearing, now just a wide expanse of drifting snow. Without trees to filter and divert it, the snow had piled deeper here. It reached to the middle of their thighs, walking through it was like wading in half-frozen molasses.

Halfway across, they stopped. They had seen someone. A gray man who so blended with the murky, motile background that only with concentration could they distinguish his silhouette against it. He carried a Henry repeater and wore a heavy fur cloak that was colorless in the gloom.

Mansell felt a warm burst of relief. "Hello!" he called. He waved his arm above his head. "Can you help us!"

The figure stood unmoving, as silent as the snow that nearly hid him.

"Hello!" Mansell called again. "How far are we from Jerusalem Camp?"

There was a long silence. Then a deep voice said, "Near."

"Praise be. Which way?"

Another long pause, then, "You pilgrims lost?"

Some fast-rising instinct kept Mansell from answering. But his partner said, "Yes. Bad lost. Which way?"

The figure edged forward two steps. They could see his outline a bit more clearly now, but the dashing flakes blurred the details of his face. Only his wind-whipped beard, long and gray, was clearly visible. "Bad place for men to be lost," he said.

"Which way to Jerusalem Camp?" repeated Mansell, fighting a peculiar urge to back away.

The man waved to his right. "Beyond that rise."

"Thank you." They pulled their horses southward a few yards. Joe stopped and turned. The Gray Man remained as before.

"Are you going there, too?"

He didn't answer or move.

Mansell said, "You could freeze out here."

"I won't freeze. I can warm myself any moment in the fires of hell."

Mansell, amazed at the singular comment, wondered if the man was insane. But it was nearly dark: urgency compelled him to move. He and Joe struggled to the rise and looked across in the remaining feeble light. They saw no town. Nothing but wild, snowbound wilderness fading into gray nonentity.

"What the . . ." Mansell muttered. He turned. The Gray Man had followed them, but remained several yards behind. "Are you sure this is the way?"

"You will reach the town," the man said. "That I promise."

"But there's nothing there."

"I will send you to the town. I know it well. It is only just now beginning to know me."

Mansell looked at the sky. It was the color of slate and growing darker. A burst of panic constricted his throat.

"Who are you?"

The old man smiled and came toward him. "Who are you?" Mansell demanded again, backing away, cold hands vainly fumbling for his weapon as the old man, still smiling, bore down upon them with the Henry upraised.

Chapter 2

Ceaselessly the snow fell from clouds that blocked the stars and moon and made the night black as a cavern. As the people of Jerusalem Camp huddled by their fires, sheets of white covered the mountain passes. Heaps of snow piled thickly on evergreen branches, making them strain, then break. Massive limbs crashed earthward, across narrow paths and wagon roads that would accommodate no travelers from now until spring. High on the notch-shaped pass that was the only route out of the basin in which Jerusalem Camp lay, the snow lay especially deep, as it did there every winter, blocking the trail and turning the pass into a natural trap where avalanches were easily triggered.

The stranger slid for the second time into sluggish awareness. He lay in semidarkness, hurting all over. Tough rope bound his wrists and ankles. He was cold and very confused.

"I had to tie you up, what with how you went at us before," a voice said. "My name's Jared Cable. I'm a blacksmith. Town marshal, too." The speaker's face came into focus. Smiling but stern, it was the face of a strong man. One the stranger had seen when he had come to the first time.

The tied man strained at his bonds. "Cut these ropes."

"I can't. I don't blame you for flying off like you did, the way Rupert and the gang knocked you out. But until I know you're going to stay calm, I can't cut you loose."

"Why am I being treated like a criminal?"

"Because there's been two murders in this valley this past week. First in its history. Everybody's scared. Maybe that didn't give nobody the right to jump you, but jump you they did. And I might as well ask you, why were those riders gunning after you?"

"I owe you no explanations."

"No. But if you don't talk, you'll spend the rest of the winter tied in that bed."

The stranger exhaled slowly, frowning. Finally he said, "They were trying to rob me, I think. Followed me in from the foothills. You going to cut me loose now?"

"I might. What brought you to Jerusalem Camp?"

"My business, not yours."

"What's your name?"

"Not your business either."

Jared scratched his day-old beard. "All right. Suit yourself." He turned toward the door.

"You're leaving me like this?"

"You ain't cooperating, friend."

The prisoner glared bitterly at him. Finally he said, "I came here just to be coming. No reason. That's the truth. My name's Tellico."

"Tellico who?"

"Tellico's sufficient."

So, Tellico's sufficient, you rode in to the mountains at the front end of a blizzard—for no reason?"

"That's right. Now cut these ropes and I'll ride again."

"I'm afraid you won't," Jared said. "This town is snowed in. Funny thing about the lay of our land: The valley's like a bottle, with the pass being the spout. Once snow corks it, you don't get out again." Jared produced a knife and began sawing at Tellico's ropes.

"What's this about murder?"

"Two so far. Man name of Davison and his boy, both out in the mountains when it happened. You picked a bad time to ride in to Jerusalem Camp."

Tellico stood with difficulty, rubbing his wrists. He went to a window and threw back the burlap curtain. Snow pelted the pane, flakes frozen so hard they rattled the glass. He laughed ironically. "Snowed in, in a murder town."

"That's the size of it." Jared said.

Tellico turned and gave Jared his best chance yet to view him. His hair was sandy, slightly long and rather unruly. His eyes an intense green. His skin was ruddy and fair, though a heavy undergrowth of whiskers somewhat darkened his cheeks. He was slender but far from frail, and seemed tense as a fiddle string.

His shirt was blue, his trousers made of heavy, slightly greasy canvas, his boots well worn and devoid of ornamentation. When they had captured him he had been wearing a gun belt with a Remington tucked into it. Rupert had taken it, but Jared had reconfiscated it from him.

"Am I a prisoner?" Tellico asked.

"Only of snow and circumstancees. I've got no reason to hold you, as long as you keep yourself out of trouble."

"All right."

"What are you going to do with yourself? You got any means of support?"

The question, strangely, made Tellico laugh. "I've been asking myself that very question for some time now," he said. "But I'll survive. If I get hungry I can hunt."

"You're taking being trapped here mighty well. Especially given the circumstances. There are those who won't think it a coincidence that you came in at the same time two people got murdered."

"I'll be careful."

"I won't lie to you, Tellico. I'll be watching you myself. I find you a believable man, somehow. But I can't believe any man rides into a wilderness like this, at a time like this, for no reason."

Also by Elmer Kelton:

THE MAN WHO RODE MIDNIGHT

Winner of the 1988 Western Heritage Award For Best Novel

☐ 27713 $3.50

Bantam is pleased to offer these other exciting Western adventures from ELMER KELTON, one of the great Western storytellers with a special talent for capturing the fiercely independent spirit of the West:

☐ 27351 HORSEHEAD CROSSING $2.95
☐ 27119 LLANO RIVER $2.95
☐ 27218 MANHUNTERS $2.95
☐ 27620 HANGING JUDGE $2.95
☐ 27467 WAGONTONGUE $2.95

BANTAM
SHOP·AT·HOME
C·A·T·A·L·O·G

Special Offer
Buy a Bantam Book
for only 50¢.

Now you can have Bantam's catalog filled with hundreds of titles plus take advantage of our unique and exciting bonus book offer. A special offer which gives you the opportunity to purchase a Bantam book for only 50¢. Here's how!

By ordering any five books at the regular price per order, you can also choose any other single book listed (up to a $5.95 value) for just 50¢. Some restrictions do apply, but for further details why not send for Bantam's catalog of titles today!

Just send us your name and address and we will send you a catalog!

★ WAGONS WEST ★

A series of unforgettable books that trace the lives of a dauntless band of pioneering men, women, and children as they brave the hazards of an untamed land in their trek across America. This legendary caravan of people forge a new link in the wilderness. They are Americans from the North and the South, alongside immigrants, Blacks, and Indians, who wage fierce daily battles for survival on this uncompromising journey—each to their private destinies as they fulfill their greatest dreams.

☐	26822	INDEPENDENCE! #1	$4.50
☐	26162	NEBRASKA! #2	$4.50
☐	26242	WYOMING! #3	$4.50
☐	26072	OREGON! #4	$4.50
☐	26070	TEXAS! #5	$4.50
☐	26377	CALIFORNIA! #6	$4.50
☐	26546	COLORADO! #7	$4.50
☐	26069	NEVADA! #8	$4.50
☐	26163	WASHINGTON! #9	$4.50
☐	26073	MONTANA! #10	$4.50
☐	26184	DAKOTA! #11	$4.50
☐	26521	UTAH! #12	$4.50
☐	26071	IDAHO! #13	$4.50
☐	26367	MISSOURI! #14	$4.50
☐	27141	MISSISSIPPI! #15	$4.50
☐	25247	LOUISIANA! #16	$4.50
☐	25622	TENNESSEE! #17	$4.50
☐	26022	ILLINOIS! #18	$4.50
☐	26533	WISCONSIN! #19	$4.50
☐	26849	KENTUCKY! #20	$4.50
☐	27065	ARIZONA! #21	$4.50
☐	27458	NEW MEXICO! #22	$4.50

Prices and availability subject to change without notice.

- -

A Proud People in a Harsh Land

THE SPANISH BIT SAGA

Set on the Great Plains of America in the early 16th century, Don Coldsmith's acclaimed series recreates a time, a place and a people that have been nearly lost to history. With the advent of the Spaniards, the horse culture came to the people of the Plains. In THE SPANISH BIT SAGA we see history in the making through the eyes of the proud Native Americans who lived it.

THE SPANISH BIT SAGA
Don Coldsmith